AGNUS DEI

AGNUS DEI

Templar Knots + Krosses

Andrew David Doyle

iUniverse, Inc.
Bloomington

AGNUS DEI
Templar Knots + Krosses

iUniverse books may be ordered through booksellers or by contacting:

iUniverse
1663 Liberty Drive
Bloomington, IN 47403
www.iuniverse.com
1-800-Authors (1-800-288-4677)

ISBN: 978-1-4759-5259-9 (sc)
ISBN: 978-1-4759-5261-2 (hc)
ISBN: 978-1-4759-5260-5 (ebk)

Library of Congress Control Number: 2012918477

Printed in the United States of America

iUniverse rev. date: 10/16/2012

Acknowledgements

To the OSMTH KT, for permitting an insight into a fascinating and clandestine world.

This work is dedicated in part to my wife Susan Doyle, who has endured more than most with my incessant drive for constant review, and, more importantly for becoming a 'laptop widow' where most of a writer's time is at the qwerty.

To, Miss Robin Linn who has provided a great deal of literary oversight, not just with Agnus Dei, but also with the construction of The Silent Apostle II.

To Gary Bertie friend and colleague who supports me still, through thick and thin.

And, finally to friends and family who share the excitement of bringing all my work into the public domain.

Thank you.

Agnus Dei

'Templar-Knots ✠ Krosses'
1812-2012

By Andrew David Doyle

 The Order 1127

Hugues De Payens—Geoffrey De Saint Omer—
Andrew Montbard—Gondomar

Payen of Mondidier—Roral—Godfrey—
Geoffroy Bissot—Archambeau Saint Amand.

Ordo Supremus Militaris Templi Hierosolymitani

- Magnum Magisterium Porto -

The Order Today—2012

*The Grand Priory of Scotland is a component unit of the Order
of The Knights' Templar, a Sovereign International organisation
whose existence dates back to the first years of the 12th century.
Today the Order has fifty thousand plus members in over
forty-five countries and regularly undertakes works of charity
and support to those in need.*
'Ordre Souverain et Militaire du Temple

About the Author

Andrew David Doyle was educated in Dundee, Scotland, prior to joining the ranks of the British Army (Royal Artillery), with a successful career that stemmed almost fifteen years. After which he embarked into the commercial world of hydrocarbon exploitation and currently works globally.

Andrew enjoys his new-found hobby as an author, and has recently became a member of the Society of Authors.

Other works of a similar genre, written and published by Author.

- *The Circle of Swords 'Voyage of the Temple Unicorn'*
- *The Silent Apostle*
- *The Lost Monks of Avalon 'Avalonian Traveler's Guide'*
- *The Whispering Swordsman*
- *Agnus Dei—Knots + Krosses*

Chevalier Andrew David Doyle OSMTH KT Scotland.

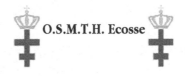

Introduction

This 'fictional' piece of work Agnus Dei—Knots & Krosses was undertaken by the author who has applied his understanding and knowledge regarding this particular institution's authority, and has executed a healthy degree of—'due diligence' toward the subject matter at hand.

The premise of this notional drama is primarily based upon the copious amount of information afforded to the author by varying sources, of which comprises of substantial detail and has been sourced, cited, and extracted from a wider range of outlets, but more importantly based on sensitive and intimate library detail relating to the Knights Templar Order in general.

Historical detail on which the 'Knights Templar Order' was founded and very much widely available, instantly accessed by employing the services of modern day technical media use such as, google, facebook, and other social media, where a vast amount of documentary evidence is in constant circulation.

The Scottish author of :—Agnus Dei 'Templar Knots + Krosses had embarked on a journey of a factual and notional nature, thus, embarked on a historical discovery trail to absorb learn and disclose some of the 'not so well known' facts and detail regarding the Knights Templar Order's modern establishment, the work is not about explaining the Order with any intended scholastic standing or disguising any esoterical messages that may have ran rife through the centuries, but a simple, interesting storyline woven together to capture what is the most intriguing society post-biblical times and to shine a little controlled light as to how the Order physically manage their modern day assets.

Agnus Dei 'Templar Knots + Krosses is dedicated to our global brothers and sisters who choose to follow the path of Christ and to the memory of the Order's founder, 'Hugues De Payens'.

Preface

The storyline that unfolds touches on items of ephemera, letters and artefacts and perhaps relics that have been shrouded in a certain mystery, and where relevant such items that legally belong to the Order may have been made available as tangible evidence for research purposes, where the author intimates that does include visits to Mdina Cathedral, St John's Co-Cathedral, Malta, and St Paul's Cathedral London & Roslin Chapel Scotland, amongst others as places to view some of the belongings of the contemporary Order.

Additional 'items' described in this work will remain;—'**as is**' and of which, will have either been discussed, reviewed and acknowledged or indeed simply fabricated by the author as part of this fictional storyline.

The research undertaken for this work was complimented by an extensive literature review and a fact finding exercise that involved journeys to. Jordan, Egypt, Malta, Norway, London & Italy and the primary location of the work—Scotland but not dismissing Germany where the author spent a considerable amount of time as a serving soldier and had visited the many other sites mentioned in this narrative.

Articles of faith: Credendum

- *Certain physical items in this work may not even exist at all, and the reader must harbour the notion is that these articles of faith remain in the realm of the reader's understanding of this book, and upon which the reader has the option to decide—what is fact and what is fiction.*

Observations and POV—point of view comments by the author are based on personal experiences by either:—viewing or researching temple pieces, or has physically handled actual ceremonial objects that adorn the Knights Templar environment.

Most of the Temple's articles of faith are physically located within cathedrals, church vaults or museums, in either Malta, Scotland Jordan, St Petersburg or Porto as examples, which are in essence managed under a strict controlled framework.

CHAPTER ONE

Knights' Templar—
The Grand Master's Notes

The two figures scurried with great haste through the quiet city streets, negotiating the inner network of tall buildings and smaller structures that formed the central city façade of old Barrack Street. The couple were hastily making their arduous way through the hidden back streets and alleyways of Dundee, looking for a safe haven in order to shelter themselves—not just from the horrendous downpour of rain, but from a contingent of fanatical Germans who were in hot pursuit of them and their hidden secret.

The duo were in the process of making a beeline for the obscure offices of the Order, known locally as the Fisher Kings, when they came to an abrupt halt just two hundred metres from the Fisher building's entrance. It was then that a single gunshot could be heard echoing from somewhere inside the building nearby.

Kemp Hastings, being the taller of the two, clutched a medium-sized, red, leather satchel, as if his life depended upon it, and hastily stepped backwards in anticipation that a stray bullet was making it's way inbound toward him and his partner-in-no-crime as yet, who was somewhat smaller in stature and was clearly of female build, who was struggling terribly to keep pace with the long gait of the biblical investigator. In his haste, as he was taking extra-long strides in a rather excited state of mind.

Madelyn Linn, on the other hand, was exhausted, having been literally dragged from their car and forced to sprint through three hundred puddles of shitty rainwater that lay in her non-negotiable path. And she was literally being pulled along the street by her investigative partner, feeling that she was being treated like more of a hostage as opposed to being a willing participant; subsequently being physically whipped between a million parked cars in the process.

If that was not enough for Madelyn to contend with, she was also subjected to at least three sporadic showers induced by more than a zealous set of idiot drivers who wanted to wash pedestrians as they drove by, and all that, since leaving the car park just a few hundred metres away. It was five o'clock in the morning and time was ticking on. Therefore, to coin a simple, Scottish phrase, 'it was cold and it was pishing doon with rain, and time was of the essence'.

Madelyn took a further three steps, then stopped abruptly in her tracks, momentarily tugging and pulling at Hastings' long, army style coat in desperation.

"Stop, Kemp, or at least bloody slow down you big ape will you. You are like a deranged convict escaping from Alcatraz. My short legs cannot keep up with your long, streaky legs. I am only five foot six, you know! And by the way was that gunshots I heard a moment ago?" she remarked, while still grasping with her wet gloves at his long, and extremely soaked, trench coat in a last ditch effort to hold him back a few extra seconds in order to catch her breath. Or perhaps even more so, in an effort to stop him from sprinting away entirely.

Mother Nature, in her best Scottish tradition, was just being a complete bitch and she had battered the city of Dundee for three consecutive days by sending torrents, upon torrents of rain water down on the unsuspecting city of discovery. Hastings waited a moment or two before answering Madelyn's question.

'Not sure Madelyn, but if it was then we are in some really deep shit, can you believe this bloody weather.'

He responded whilst slowly stepping back into the shadows of the doorway. A few metres away and the rain water had started to clog up the many streets and avenues, not to mention the many flood drains and support pipework that ran underground the complete length and breadth of the city, which was now, flowing to capacity as the ever increasing density of water simply added more volume to the already struggling flood and drainage system.

This was clearly an older and very out-dated water management system that was now failing again, and had begun to overflow, leaving a multitude of small pools and water puddles in almost every conceivable dip and recess, waiting to dissipate into the awaiting mass of the River Tay.

The River Tay itself being an expansive body of water that flows eastwards and meets the cold North Sea as it passes along the esplanade of the city between the counties of Angus and Fife—separated by two and a half miles of deep water and straddled by two very substantial bridges for road and rail crossings.

The rain puddles were a certain nightmare for anyone trying to walk the aquatic streets, let alone attempting to run their full length at any increased pace. Hastings turned and paused for thought then eventually spun a full 360 degrees in order to face Madelyn. It was then that he realised what a complete arse he had just been.

"Sorry, Darlene, sorry, sorry. Ooops, I mean, Madelyn!"

Hastings momentarily corrected himself as he responded to his water-drenched partner whilst remaining mindful that Darlene Gammay was in the process of re-arranging her complete existence on the planet. The teacher, Madelyn, was removing any reference to her old self as a result of some recent life-changing experiences or biblical events that were captured by a novelist in the works of 'The Silent Apostle'. Thus having endured a certain nightmare that had left her psychologically scarred for life, and she had recently changed her name by deed poll. Hastings was continuously struggling with the name change.

The life changing event that had left her with an inexplicable tattoo spread across her back for ten days and nights with no rational explanation as to why or where the phenomenon had originated from, suffice to say she had become an inexplicable host of an religious event that was still being investigated by the Vatican.

Hastings had decided to reduce his pace down to a slower rate, obviously for the benefit of his new partner who was indeed 'only' a member of the opposite sex and was perhaps not as physically fit or indeed built as males are. But, in the main, females were said to be slightly more emotionally intelligent. He took a deep breath, and then spoke.

"We don't have much time, my dear girl. We have to secure this ledger somewhere safe, a place far away from any further interference and especially out of sight from those 'Krouts'. And, before anyone realises that this document has been removed from its once safe haven. Let alone the fact that we actually have custody of it. This is not good for our health, Madelyn! If we are not careful, we could end up in the morgue just as quick as Freddy, the curator at Restenneth Priory did. Especially now. If we are caught with this little ditty in our possession, those Germans will stop at nothing, until they have the document in their possession, and we are quite dead and pushing up the worms. They are outright, bloody fanatical about biblical things and anything to do with The Knights' Templar's ancient documents. And this bloody, damn rain is not helping us much!"

Hastings took a fleeting glance toward the churchyard, then spoke.

"But then again, Maddy, it may be just the answer to our many prayers, and perhaps could buy us a little more time." he said, and appeared to be extremely agitated and perplexed, especially since it had only been twenty-four hours since his contact in the local archive office in the Priory building had died under very suspicious circumstances indeed, and, who was apparently found clutching a 13th century protective cover flysheet, which appeared to be an older facsimile copy of a Templar inventory document.

The document in question was hailed to be one of the most recent acquisitions lists or holdings inventory belonging to the Holy Order of the Knights' Templar, and was an addendum to an ancient document dating back to at least the year 1133. But had been updated in the years 1812 and 1947, respectively, and of which, had been secreted within a library of some rather older books much earlier in history, dating nearer to the year 1681, according to the library KT reference tag '003.1415.'

Hastings was momentarily alerted by a flash of light from an upper window followed by another gunshot which sent an instant cold fear racing up through his active mind. He took another deep breath, and extracted a handkerchief from his inside jacket pocket and wiped his face, then took a long stare into the middle distance then tilted his head sidewards.

'We need to move quickly Madelyn'. He said and continued to explain why they had been caught up in this deadly game of cat and mouse. 'This document, this actual thesaurus inventory, has pages which have been neatly placed and lodged together between pages 28, 30 and 32 and of which in essence, is a book that explains how to don medieval armour in exacting detail.

The 'Templari Thesaurus' in its original format had been formally scribed by the hand and quill of no other than one Knight in particular, 'Hugues De Payens' himself, a man who was better known as the first Grand Master of the Holy Order of the Knights' Temple Saint John, circa 1128, and this is what makes it so precious.'

Madelyn pulled at the collar of her long jacket and extended it up over her neckline and then shook her head with great vigour momentarily sending tiny droplets of rainwater in all directions, apparently not paying too much close attention to Hastings in his ramblings.

She felt rather like a drowned rat, her clothes were wet, her mascara was running and her feet were drenched and very cold. She even felt chilled down to her very inner core, and was by any stretch of the imagination extremely pissed off, and wanted a cup of tea more than anything else she could imagine on the planet at this time.

Somehow Hastings had dismissed her as a working partner and was making headway almost leaving her behind in his wake. He was on a mission from God and possessed an unhealthy drive of effort to rid himself of the deadly dossier whilst simultaneously trying to remain alive.

He grabbed Madelyn's hand and led her out of the doorway, then suddenly stopped again; he then shrugged his broad shoulders and moved forward with more of a military pose. A few moments later, they approached the crossroads junction to the east of Barrack Street and scanned the adjacent Meadowside area.

Madelyn gazed on and took a good long look at Kemp Hastings as he assessed their situation. He was easily five foot ten, strong athletic build, and had obviously been a fit and healthy soldier in his hay day. His hair was brown and wavey and cut not too short but yet not too long and very well kept. His skin tone was fresh apart from being saturated with copious droplets of rain water. As far as Madelyn was concerned this was the man of her womanly dreams.

Kemp Hastings possesses the most piercing blue eyes you could ever encounter, eyes that sent anyone he stared directly at, into an almost sexual frenzy or conversely, where his colleague was concerned heaven. His chiselled jawline and strong check bones made most good looking men turn away in acute jealousy, and he was easily a candidate for 'the groom of the year award'.

Madelyn let her daydream linger on a little bit longer, she knew him quite well, and yet although he was normally a very benign soft gentle kind of man, recent events had triggered his alter ego character to come into the forefront, and his mission was now survival. She felt somehow protected by him especially now with these echoing gunshots and hostile weather, and he had stepped in front of her to shield her from potential stray 9mm projectiles.

The rain had begun to ease up a little and was now more of a drizzle than a raging torrent. He listened intently, then waited a moment or two longer before glancing over to his left hand side. He targeted a point where the graveyard of the 15th century cemetery sat in all its grey, dull glory, and they converged at the street corner. All seemed to be quiet.

The cemetery appeared even more sinister somehow, more abandoned in time than he had remembered. It resembled a grey scene that could be easily described as a location found within a Mary Shelley novel—the Victorian look of despair and desperation about it. The last time he had reasons to venture beyond the deathly gates was in a bit more of a relaxed atmosphere whilst paying his respects to the dearly departed. Now it was very different especially with an unscheduled visit to the field of the dead, which was completely different under this veil of secrecy, and could be deemed almost traumatic.

He motioned Madelyn to wait under another doorway and urged her take refuge from the inclement weather, just as he tucked the soft red satchel further up under his great coat, then moved into a better position to observe the not-so-busy street.

He then glanced to his right side again, gazing over and across the main thoroughfare. It was relatively quiet apart from streams of water dribbling off the rooftops and cascading down over the many roofs and bonnets of the few parked cars that sat on the street. He then glanced off to his left and was staring directly at the Fisher King's doorway entrance.

It was then that he spied the red BMW parked awkwardly at the entranceway. The car had been fitted with an odd numbered licence plate. The vehicle itself having been parked half on the pavement and half on the roadway which appeared to be a haphazard attempt at parking. It looked cumbersome and the vehicle's driver was awkwardly shifting in his seat. The vehicle's hazard lights were flashing away to warn of its presence and he noticed the engine was still running—perhaps the driver was pending a quick getaway.

Hastings pulled himself back slightly into the cover of the shadows just out of sight of the driver, and observed from a safer distance just in case all was not as he wished for. The one occupant of the vehicle still unaware that Hasting's was less than fifty feet away and was in possession of something the driver would apparently quite easily kill for. His colleague had taken a corner position behind him and was using him as a kind of human shield, her Knight in not so shining armour.

Hastings had one of those uncanny gut instincts that somehow had alerted him. He just knew this was bad news as his gut flinched uncontrollably and he momentarily gulped a cold, hard globule of spit. He was sure that he had observed the BMW before, but thought it was an unmarked police car at first, and then he dismissed this notion having spied the foreign number plate. It was an Italian registered car and not very inconspicuous if you were evading the authorities or trying to remain incognito.

He pinched his lips, wiped his face, then made his way back to the doorway where Madelyn was standing. He gave her a fleeting glance then noticed how vulnerable she actually looked. He suddenly froze as a single cold spike and icy shudder ran the length of his spine, he looked at her again.

She was busy trying to do something constructive with her long hair, but it was futile, she looked a right proper state he instantly thought, then smiled unconvincingly at her. He knew deep down this was going to cost him dearly.

Her hair was dripping rain water and the many strands of her blonde locks had draped over her beautiful face, clinging in desperation to hide her young female looks. She was obviously cold and was shivering uncontrollably. He instantly felt guilty of treating her like a piece of additional luggage and placed an arm around her shoulders to comfort her, then he spoke.

'My goodness, Madelyn, I am so sorry. I have dragged you through the streets like a used shopping trolley, and in this damn rain too, don't worry though I will make it up to you, honest, I will, I promise. Hey, look at me! Smile, you look great! But for now let's secure this little treasure first, then, we can get the hell out of here and get something to warm us up. It's not safe to go into the FK building.

I feel they may have already had some unwelcome visitors and I do not think they were collecting the rent either, well, not just at this particular moment in time. Now c'mon, follow me, we must hide this inventory elsewhere. And I think I may just know the perfect place, over there Dr Linn—let's go!" He exclaimed and pointed toward the graveyard entrance across the street.

"We can hide the parchment in there; look no-one would ever look for a book in a graveyard now, would they? You can pick any grave you wish young Madelyn. There are over two hundred and ninety to choose from".

He asked her again, then started walking quickly toward the entrance and almost slid through the stone walled gateway into the cemetery as his black leather brogues lost traction underfoot sending him into a moment of instability. With Madelyn in tow, he quickly recovered from his slip with the assistance of his partner and they made their way to the southern end of the bone yard.

Hastings was still looking and searching for a specific grave marker. He knew that there was one grave in particular that lay in one of the many avenues of the dead, and all he had to do was locate it.

The many tiered avenues of gravestones stood like soldiers on parade. Of course a few were not so quite orderly, given the amount of time they had stood silent on the hallowed parade square. He counted thirty-two stones going south, followed by twenty-seven similar stones traversing east, and then he stood motionless opposite his single target epitaph.

He respectfully nodded and acknowledged that the slab appeared even more sinister or sadder than the rest. As the rain continued to drizzle down over its main panel, he glanced at the adjacent stones: many were covered with a sea of green weed which had eaten into the crumbling concrete, a range of epitaphs of the ancient grave markers sadly being eaten by Mother Nature.

"Have you picked a grave yet, Maddy? Don't worry, I found what I was looking for, sorry, but pick one anyway. It will help you later to find our drop box, over there the one with the grizzly face on it," he said, pointing to a marker stone with no writing or names to decipher, just an effigy that said it all—an indicator to those who knew what the symbols of the Holy Order actually meant. He was, in essence, looking for a 'real time dead letter box' but in this case, a single grave that had been engraved with a figurine face of the 'Green Man'.

The headstone of the 'GM' was located exactly where he was told, five rows up, and one stone in, sitting a few metres to the left of the witch stone and just sitting off the chipped walkway, and could be very easily located for his next intended visit in the darkness of night. 'Or, even in the worst case scenario, if his successor was to follow in his dear, departed footsteps, and that would be the very worst case scenario, indeed', he thought.

"That should do nicely!" he mumbled.

"No one will ever find it in there, what do you think?"

He asked her again, waiting for a reply.

"If you think so," replied Madelyn, who still had more important issues with her hair than thinking about the location of the gravestone.

Hastings then got down on his hands and knees and started to scrape back a few handfuls of very wet mud away from the top of the grassy mound. He then extracted the highly desirable 'Thesaurus Inventory' from the satchel and buried the plastic covered vellum under a few inches of the brown, slimy top layer of sludge. He then grabbed a fistful of grass and began to camouflage over his handiwork.

Madelyn, meanwhile, gazed over the cemetery expecting to see ghosts and ghouls flirting about the yard of the departed and making their way between the many 15th and 16th century headstones, but, obviously none did. She felt very uneasy and somehow knew they were being watched and felt somehow vulnerable again.

She glanced up at the old city grey walled buildings and began quizzing the many edifices, windows and ventilation recesses, and the range of unaligned architecture that overlooked the graveyard. She was looking for voyeurs or people who were spying on their impromptu strange activity.

She leaned over a small hedge and picked up three yellow daffodils out of a nearby glass urn and placed them on top of the stone belonging to the Green Man, just as Hastings added the finishing touches to the wet mud mound.

She looked up again, having thought that by placing some flowers on the gravestone it would somehow indicate to anyone watching that they were simply paying their respects to the dearly departed, albeit, it was still odd that two people would walk through a bone yard at five in the morning, and in the torrential flood rains to boot. But nevertheless, people still do the oddest of things in the rain.

She noticed that many windows had either been blacked out by paint, or had been cement-stoned over. A couple of windows however were very ornate and appeared out of place amongst the older style and contemporary building designs. That was before she realised that the building's edifice was the back office windows to the Fisher Kings building and had somehow been carved with a more ornate facia.

She thought for another moment then gave herself a psychological kick, having again found herself caught up on another unusual sort of quest along with her newly found business partner Kemp Hastings—after swearing she would avoid any more ludicrous or ad hoc adventures with him. And now look. Then realised how wrong she was.

However, in order to pay the daily bills they would sometimes undertake missions of investigations on the understanding of whoever paid them enough for their efforts, but even more so employ them as specialists, in their given fields. Madelyn, being a Biblical Historian who could decipher the most ancient of documents and possessed an unlimited access to the academic world.

Kemp Hastings, on the other hand, was a private investigator of antiquities and strange occurrences, who incidentally had some great drinking buddies and had studied a little. Both of them having been brought together on this occasion to investigate the hidden archives of the Knights' Templar Order, and had both been commissioned under the pretence of conducting a comprehensive internal audit.

It had appeared that the Order had lost track of its many assets, and in a concerted attempt to search locate and provide an approximate actual inventory, they would have to go to extra ordinary lengths to achieve this outcome, if they wished to close the inventory off in the next twelve months or so for insurance purposes.

The Order decided to employ the pair and they were soon commissioned on behalf of the Holy Order—The Knights' Templar, Scotland. The recent lawmakers had made life difficult for any establishment to procure and maintain wealth over the hundred million pounds mark, and the Order were increasingly worried that they might have to split the family silver down even further for financial declaration.

The couple were then provided with open access to the Order's public archives. As part of their primary mission they were also tasked to try and locate and record the whereabouts of a single parchment known simply as:

'De' Templari Thesaurus'

The actual thesaurus document was last officially reviewed, between circa 1804 and 1812, and was hailed to have been updated by two of the Order's Grand Masters, Alexander Deuchar and Admiral Sir David Milne, during their tenures as CEO's of the rather well-established, non-profit and charitable organisation.

But, for some unknown reason, the outgoing Grand Master had secreted the document within an obscure set of library documents relating to books about donning medieval armour.

It was not until December 2011, whilst the documents were still housed in Mdina on the island of Malta, when they were re-discovered by mistake. The documents back then were controlled and captured under the umbrella of care by the St John's chief archivist, who again, for some strange reason deliberately placed the books out of circulation.

The books eventually forming part of an archive overspill ended up in Restenneth Priory—in Scotland, as opposed to being donated to a local academic establishment in Europe.

The original 'Primo di Templari Thesaurus' or 'vault inventory' was a list that was said to contain the secret details of a comprehensive wealth inventory: comprising of artefacts, documents, treasures, gold bullion and holy relics. The document was also annotated with the names of the inventory's 19th and 20th century custodians.

The intrinsic detail of which was coupled with a series of succession plans and contemporary locations of where the Order's local wealth was actually stored or physically hidden. The inventory was also endorsed by the current Grand Master of the day, along with a future procurement strategy.

It was easy, therefore, to see why these precious bits of paper were so popular and even today people were already lining up to procure them, even if it meant certain death.

The existence of the 'Templari Thesaurus' again, came to light to historical archivists in early June 1944, when the so-called treasure seekers of post War Britain and the Fatherland were chasing the stolen wealth that was acquired by the Germans during World War II, specifically.

Whereupon, a single Teutonic Monk, known as 'Klaus Kornatt', had stumbled across six parchments that were neatly tucked into a series of books relating to medieval armour and warfare tactics; the books belonging to a discarded batch which had been identified and marked for 'disposal' in the old library.

The Teutonic Monk, Klaus, in his duties as a scribe, apparently had dismissed the actual endorsed letters as mere internal handling notes, of which basically formed a series of identification and custodial documents, signatures, lists and dates and simple information that mapped the lifecycle of a book.

A further example being library cards, but maintained within a slightly more complex 'T'-Card system, and yet the Monk had simply sent the documents to Switzerland in early August of 1944.

It was during the post war era that a special investigation was also initiated by the Order to assist local Governments in sourcing the vast amounts of lost, stolen or forgotten war trophies, and, as a matter of course in particular the 'German spoils of War' whereupon, again, the Vatican and the Knights were desperate to be repatriated with their many holy relics.

The Knights' Order was more than aware that the Deutsche spoils of war contained a range of serious biblical relics and art works painted by the many masters. Items that the Order and the Vatican had once held as relics and was deemed lost, as Hitler's henchmen raped Europe of its social, historical and artistic identity.

It was through the process of elimination, regarding the whereabouts of where these relics ended up, that exposed a series of inexplicable or very strange events which came to light just after the war had ended. Events which fuelled rumours about the actual whereabouts of the Third Reich coffers, or portions of the Reichsbank 400 million dollar gold deposits.

The booty was said to have consisted of several thousand gold bars or approximately 7.3 Billion dollars in today's commercial market value, and several hundred coffers of 'Deutsche Reichsbank' coinage, and a huge, single batch of booty which had simply seemed to vanish off the face of the planet, disappearing somewhere between Southern Germany, Austria, Scotland or England or, at best guess, them all.

And, if current rumours were to be believed then many indicators were pointing towards the current safe havens, ranging from the deepest and darkest and certainly colder waters, as far off within Scotland's many lochs, or conversely, lying closer to Hitler's Eagles nest home in Bavaria, submerged to the sandy bottom of Lake Toplitz, or simply sitting amongst other sunken treasures in the surrounding lochs across Austria.

Hastings meanwhile had stood up and was quizzing the stone walled gateway. He spied a flash of red as the car took off at some haste. Heading away from the Bank Street road junction, the vehicle momentarily appeared to slow down just outside the perimeter wall opposite the central gateway, then sped off.

As he stared at his handiwork, he heard another noise, it was another loud rev of the car's diesel engine and the BMW was hastily making its way toward the easterly junction; after which a quick squeal of the brakes could be distinctly heard as a stray dog suddenly ran from the doorway of a nearby shop, and headed across the road causing the driver to brake sharply.

Hastings momentarily grabbed Madelyn and pulled her downwards with one quick jerk of her arm, sending her head completely head over heels in the process. She had ended up sitting in a small pool of watery, brownish mud behind the headstone of the Green Man epitaph.

As she gazed up, it took a few seconds before realising what she was actually staring at. She then jumped unexpectedly, finding herself confronted by the stone face or more of an effigy of an actual larger-than-life sized man's face, the carving being encrusted with copious amounts of branches and twigs, bearing all sorts of fruits coming out of his mouth.

After her little scare, she acknowledged that the image was cleverly carved and had been strategically designed into the mason work to represent the evolution of the seasons and appeared almost ghoulish or gruesome, but menacing nonetheless.

"Shit! Shit! Shit!" she exclaimed, very loudly.

"That's it, Kemp, enough is enough. I have just about had a gut full of this . . . Sh . . ." Then she shot him the most disgusted look a scorned woman could muster.

Hastings, meanwhile, was still down on bended knees; he just grinned back at her then placed a single finger over her mouth and shook his head.

"Shhh, not now, Madelyn, not now! Please, please any other bloody time but not right now, our lives are at stake here!"

Madelyn seemed to have calmed down a little bit then moved to one side of the grave stone as she watched the BMW move off and cross over the junction, where the car then disappeared out of her view.

Hastings had assumed that the two occupants of the vehicle remained oblivious as to their whereabouts and were unaware that the investigator and Miss Linn had entered the quiet surroundings of the inner city's resting place of the dead.

As far as Hastings and Madelyn were concerned, they were caught up in a more serious game of hide and seek, or cat and mouse, hiding and evading from an almost unknown enemy and were involved in a deadly game that could result in both their violent slaughter. And to add insult to injury, who were both currently lurking in an 16th century cemetery under the blanket of the most inhospitable weather conditions that Mother Nature could provide, and there were no rules to abide by.

"Okay, Madelyn! The coast is clear—they are gone," he remarked, whilst turning around to face her and chat. But to his horror, she was not there, she had gone. It was just a stroke of sheer luck that he spied her making her way back out of the cemetery gates and was making her way onto the not-so-busy street.

Hastings gave chase and caught her up just in the nick of time, and instantly made the assumption that she was one hundred per cent adamant in her angry, cold state that she was about to march headlong into the office buildings of the Fisher Kings.

"No, no, no, Madelyn, what do you think you are you doing, you silly girl? We are too late to visit the Fishers, trust me, this feels so wrong. Something is definitely not quite right here. We should get the hell out of here and bloody quickly."

Madelyn stared back at him and started to shake her head. Kemp took a deep breath then stopped.

'Madelyn, the Fisher Kings are what we call an absolute establishment, they represent the lineage of Jesus Christ or the protection of that notion, in this modern world, we Agnus Dei—Lamb of God are exactly from the same core breed but, we have what you would call a closer link to the reality of the esoteric Church

Literally speaking, if you accept that Jesus was the lamb of God, a physical man who took away the sins of the world and eventually was triumphant over death. A man who won the day for the persecuted, that's fine by me, but right now, this very minute, I do not wish to join his cause so early in the day now let's get out of here.

Now, you are a biblical studies type of person, you work it out, I have been trying to for years, but one thing to me is very clear, I know that I belong to an institution that demands a certain level of sacrifice for perpetuity and that is why I am a man on a mission, and that mission maybe even be directed from God himself, if you want to think metaphorically.

The two then stared at one another then started to walk back to their car.

CHAPTER TWO

Dead Letter box

Hastings had already started his investigation and begun his audit trail. He had recently visited the home of one of the Order's older custodians and Grand Constables. Dr Norman Niven Airlie, a local chapel cleric, who strangely flirted between two or three actual churches in Angus and Fife and various other locations across middle Scotland in his duty as a Temple custodian.

Hastings thought that the cleric was a strange kind of man, and would never have placed him so senior in the Order, let alone anticipate where he was placed today in modern society. Hastings sat opposite the old man, then leaned over the coffee table and stared into the eyes of the old cleric. Dr Niven possessed the eyes of a very wise old man indeed; his piercing gaze left Hastings with an odd sort of awkward feeling, an uncanny emotional displacement as if he was intruding into the old man's affairs and business, which, by default was what he was really doing.

The cleric of God smiled back at him, then spoke. "Not easy to get one's head around the full complexity of such an establishment is it? The Order is so multifaceted, so complex that there are simply too many layers of protection to break down into logical chunks. Too many segments to attack the establishment to leave any lasting impression, well at least with any significance. Remember, Mr Hastings, this institution has almost eight hundred years of operational expertise to get its house in order."

Hastings interjected and took a sip of his sweet tea. "I have found that the many sub-offices or preceptories have a team or conclave between six to eight local members, and that each subordinate is responsible for their particular role in that specific team.

I suppose in general terms that, in essence, means gentlemen like your good self are, custodians of great wealth, and maintain an overarching view of the Order from within. Of course from a business context it would be likened to a local shop in a village, perhaps, ranging to a larger complex of shops in a large city and probably upwards to a local or regional outlet such as the Vatican or a host of substantial castles or a conglomerate of smaller businesses, stemming to a global chain of hypermarkets to a significant standing at country level. Something along those lines?"

The old man leaned forward and shook his head. "In the case of the Order we are talking about a global standing, so a simple organisation chart to cover a specific country is fine. But when you consider the many countries and the multi-language and socio demographics involved, it all gets rather a bit messy. So the Order places an ultimate authority and responsibility on the local Grand Priors to keep their local offices in temple Order."

The old man was mesmerised, he had been thinking a couple of thousand people, but in essence the Order were talking historical membership stemming into hundreds and thousands of Knights and Dames over the centuries.

"The enormity of membership of which is increasing into the twenty first century and is being enhanced as we speak; increasingly being populated with the advent of Dames and postulates reaching out for affiliation at most opportunities."

The old man laughed loudly. "So what are you asking me exactly, Mr Hastings? I get the impression that you are searching for answers that I may not know. But I will tell you that there are powers afoot that even the most rehearsed and wisest members of the Order still do not fully understand. Here in Scotland we are slightly different, we are a smaller unit and have a more impact on the Order, and perhaps more potency. You see, we are working to an internal framework as to how we conduct our business, we have discipline beyond discipline, we exude national identity beyond those of similar countries in size, but, our pride as a nation is a powerful tool when fighting the modern day antagonists.

And I hear we are talking about splitting up the union of Great Britain today—a sign of the times. Well, I can't say I can blame the people if they have been subject to so much open bigotry over the many hundreds of years and it's not a wonder why the people want to stand alone. I don't think separation has hurt the other countries who have managed to placate themselves from this heavy one sided rule."

The cleric picked up a leaf of paper and laid it reverently on top of the George Washington box and walked toward a rickety rocking chair and sat down. After a heavy sigh, he beckoned Hastings to take a pew. And he did mean a real pew, sitting in the window recess was a wooden, ornate church pew, constructed in heavy cedar wood and adorned with a set of the most beautiful carvings of exquisite roses and cherubs he had ever encountered.

The cleric waved his hand in the air in no particular fashion. "The throne and seat of the church, a simple church pew at any time, but place a Pope or a King upon that simple pedestal, and they become more dynamic and worldly.

They become men amongst men and yet the seat is still a seat. Yes, I remember when a very young man sat on that very pew when it was in Dresden. Yes, Mr Hastings, Dresden, Germany. An obscure little wooden pew with little standing in a normal everyday chapel. Of course this particular seat hails from the world of our current papal representative the Pope himself.

He had acquired it twenty-eight years ago, but it was given to him during his rise in the church, today a religious artefact. But here's the funny bit: it was rescued from an online auction called, gum tree, a bloody auction for goodness sake. A household servant was tasked to clear the old lodgings. Articles of faith ripped from the jaws of faith and sold to the highest bidder at an auction."

The cleric motioned Hastings to open the seat top and look inside. After a few seconds, Hastings was staring into an empty void, thinking, 'What a unique commode the chair would make', as the old man shuffled in his chair behind him.

"Slide it along, left to right. West to east, pillar to pillar c'mon Mister Hastings you know the script, but please be careful though, it is spring loaded."

Hastings managed to get his fingers into the small recess and slid the panel open. He then stood in awe as to what was sitting neatly in the middle of the pew staring back at him.

He leaned into the wooden pocket and extracted one of the biggest gold crucifixes he had ever held. It was easy twelve inches at the cross bar and at least eighteen inches on the main shaft and he guessed probably weighed at least four kilograms in weight. Hastings did a quick financial calculation based on his earlier maths for the gold contained in a suit of Grand Master's armour in his head.

"Wow, that's a cool market value of shhhhhoot!One hundred and sixty thousand pounds, cold hard cash."

It was then that Niven sneezed and Hastings flinched.

"It's not all to do with money, Mr Hastings, it is protecting the wealth of history the inventory of the Order. We know how much it costs in financial terms but what about its high intrinsic value? We are talking beyond compare here, but a token of worship where people who have little belongings or nothing by the way of material things, all they have is their faith.

We give them something to grasp on to. That is what we protect! So, yes, another item for inclusion into your valuable inventory list it may well be, but think carefully about the reason why it was constructed in the first place, and, as we have just seen, that gold crucifix saved by the grace of God having sat in that pew on its many travels. Some things are just meant to be. Imagine if any of the owners or unwise custodians knew what sat under their butts as they sat and showed people how nice the pew looked." The cleric gave out a splurt of both laughter and a hail of sneezing.

Hastings placed the cross back into its box and slid the panel back into place. Then stared back at the old man; his thoughts were certainly mixed.

After a couple of hours of discussion and a cursory walk around the cleric's modest dwelling, he then said his goodbyes and left the old man to 'die' in his bout of uncontrollable sneezing.

CHAPTER THREE

Bullets and Bullion

As Hastings and Madelyn started making their way back to the car park, a lone figure of a grey man appeared at the distant doorway. Hastings had stared back at the building as a fleeting final glance just as the figure began propping itself up against the glass panel of the inner doorway.

The figure was one of a tallish man, clad in a long trench-type overcoat and clearly struggling to stay in the upright position. Hastings quickly made his way back toward the figure, dragging the good Doctor behind him, and eventually managed to grab the man just in the nick of time as he fell forwards.

The man appeared to be in his mid-fifties and had wisps of grey hair amongst a batch of longer thick brown locks that shielded half his face. He also held two brown canvas bags which appeared to have been awkwardly stuffed under his army great coat, and he struggled to retain them as he fell down on to the stone-cold, wet slabs, now, assisted by Hastings. It was then that Hastings noticed a single patch of red blood on his jacket and the tiny droplets mixed with the water on the concrete standing.

The injured man then coughed, spluttered and then muttered a few incomprehensible, gargled words—almost managing to splurt a few coherent murmurs.

"Must . . . return back to the order, the Temple at . . . ."

The dying man coughed again just as his head fell backwards and his eyes had started rolling. Hastings held the man's head as far forward as much as he dared, just as Madelyn was feverishly trying to administer first aid by stemming the blood flow from the open wound in his chest by placing one of Hasting's handkerchiefs over the wound and pressing hard.

The gentleman appeared to have been shot at close range from the front as the blood splatter droplets appeared to be contained to a very small area of his torso, of which, had obviously left an exit wound in his back where Hastings dared not touch again, especially having felt the size of the exit wound as he lay the man down.

The stranger then fell into a bout of uncontrollable bodily spasms then spluttered a few more gargled, jargoned verbs and then spoke in an almost comprehensible gargling of words to the tune of: "The Temple . . . are . . . at kirrieeemuir, must give coins to Grand . . . Prior, he will know what to do, please . . . contact: Cameron de . . . Souza Pinto McGre . . . Order of St John . . ."

The shot man's head slowly fell backwards again and he stopped breathing. Hastings lay the man down in the emergency recovery position and looked at Madelyn.

"C'mon we need to get as far away from here as we possibly can. Hurry, we can call an ambulance on the way."

Hastings picked up one of the brown bags and handed it to the Doctor. He then grabbed the other larger bag, meanwhile doing a quick search and scan of the man's jacket pockets, he found and removed a small black wallet and stashed it into his own jacket's inside pocket.

Three hours later Kemp Hastings and Dr Linn were staring at 1,127 solid gold coins that showed indications that they could have come from a World War II mystery theft, a crime that was said to be part of this so called 7.2 billion dollar haul, and one of the most unsolved wartime crimes of the 20th century.

A single consignment of gold that was never recorded, or was ever documented as being found or disposed of, or simply closed out by any of the agencies who kept such sensitive inventories, one such inventory of National importance was held and controlled by the joint American British authorities.

The remaining gold and other war spoils of war had simply disappeared off the wartime radar map. Now, this particular clutch of gold coins signified to Hastings that this 'lot' was probably removed by one of Hitler's henchman, and was perhaps stashed as his own little hoard for post war survival, or conversely, it was simply secured by the Teutonic (German) Order.

Madelyn picked up a single coin and read the surface engraving. It read: Reichsbank Gold 5 Deutsche.

"Wow, that's an impressive coin! And they are heavy too. I wonder how much these things weigh?" she questioned, whilst picking up a clutch of smaller coins and weighing the coins in the palm of her hand.

Then she pursed her lips. "But, Hastings listen, notional thinking aside—you do know what these coins really are don't you?" she paused, then picked up a small piece of paper as she posed her question to Hastings—she remained expectant of an answer.

"This is real time Nazi gold, and not just any run-of-the-mill gold. I think this is part of a massive haul of German riches that went missing in the 1940's. But the problem I see or what I think the underlying question is . . ." She then paused again. "How on God's earth did they get here to Scotland? Because I know for a fact that the records of World War II show specifically that a Colonel Pfeiffer of the Wehrmacht was instrumental in procuring and hiding almost 736 specific crates of riches, and had somehow managed to lose 36 of them in his custodial duties, prior to jetting off to Hungary, post Blitzkreig. And that the Wehrmacht, in 1938 through to 1945, were absolutely ruthless under Hitler's insane and volatile tenure and had amassed great wealth as the tyrant leader sent legions of troops and archaeologists across the globe to procure the holiest of artefacts, relics and documents which were normally acquired at gunpoint or under the pain or certain threat of death'

Hastings was quite impressed by her sudden knowledge of global wealth and quizzed her further. She smiled and continued her own recital of post war study.

'Hitler, and his war machine, had become the ultimate fanatic on the subject and stopped at nothing in his drive for world domination—it was an unstoppable obsession.

- Thesaurus—is defined as: treasure, horde/store room, or treasury
- Templari—is defined as: Belonging to the Order of Knights' Templar

And I know this because I wrote a thesis on Jewish history a few years back and this was part of my literature review.'

Hastings just smiled back at her very nonchalantly and said nothing. Madelyn smirked and was thinking that 'silence was the stern, informed reply'. Then she watched on as Hastings played with several other gold coins, then searched the bags for any further indications that could provide them with any valuable clues.

She tipped the bag fully upside down and soon came across a small parchment of paper which had been crunched up, and a single button from a German Officer's uniform. She slowly unwrapped the paper and laid it out flat on the table top.

"Look here, Kemp, I think this could be a receipt. You don't happen to speak German by any chance do you?"

Hastings leaned forward and read the receipt. It was a receipt alright or a quittung for a single grab'-stein dated May 1946.

Hastings quizzed the paper work then commented on his findings.

"Madelyn, this is a receipt for, would you believe, a single, granite gravestone. Goodness, who on God's good earth would want to keep a receipt for a bloody headstone? Let alone stick it in a bag of gold coins sixty odd years ago—unless they wanted it to be found later of course."

It was then that the penny, sort of, dropped in his head and although he had just buried a ledger in a graveyard not too long ago, he had almost failed wholesale in his blind ignorance to comprehend that the purchase of such a plot was necessary to have control over the gravesite, and most likely the items that could potentially end up in the ground, or more simply, in the Temple's case, another marker stone.

A letter box used by a member of the holy Order to bury anything near or under it—he was back to thinking along the lines of secure, dead letter boxes and maybe another type of marker grave entirely; this time, one located in a foreign country.

The imprint address on the receipt was:

Grab stein—Bau, Haus Regli Andermatt, Nord, St Bernard, and Switz Schreib: Fur: Herrn B. Clairvaux. 05/1946—lair 2.

Hastings located a copy of his European AA road map and flicked through the pages and eventually opened it up at page 64—Switzerland. And, sure enough, he found that Andermatt was still a small village clearly defined as sitting above the great gorge known as St Bernard's pass, located on the Furka-Oberalp arterial railway route and not too far from the modern day San Gothard Tunnel.

"Great! How do you fancy a trip to Switzerland, Maddy?" He spluttered his offer whilst tapping his thighs in Swiss style dancing fashion. The Doctor was quietly sitting with her chin resting loosely in her cupped hands, and was staring back him with great interest. Although she did not appear to be too amused by his dancing antics, she did however ponder on the prospect of a few days' holiday break to Switzerland, which might just smooth things over between them.

"Tell me, Kemp." She paused. "Please tell me that you are not thinking of going off on some half-arsed, half-cocked treasure seeking trail to Switzerland now, are you?" She tutted again. "C'mon you big lump, think about it, the receipt is from the year 1946 for goodness sake. It was for a gravestone back in the 1940's, there must be a zillion grave stones in Switzerland, and simply being stuffed in a bag of gold coins does not make it an authentic article! You don't think that someone else could have just placed it in there more recently? Like our dead Fisher King guy? I mean these bags must have been emptied at some point."

Hastings smiled. 'Yes, I agree Madelyn, but, not necessarily, consider these two things first: firstly, as you know, gold is normally measured by weight, so let us say for example you just take a fistful of coins and weigh them, say ten or so, then do the actual maths. But, would you tip the complete bag upside down to see if anything else dropped out? Normally I would say yes, knowing that perhaps how many coins you were looking for?

Maybe, in this case apparently not, you see these tokens would have been kept by their keeper and only a few select people who would be permitted to see the actual coins let alone touch them. And anyway, just maybe one of them placed the receipt in the bag after the last count, who knows, maybe as a ruse or a misguiding control measure, a red herring? But I do agree it is indeed strange that the receipt is there at all.

Secondly, Andermatt, I am hoping there is only one village called Andermatt, which I know is a small rural village in the Swiss alps; a small community that contains only one graveyard as far as I can recall, a location that is quite easy to locate. And guess what, Madelyn? I have actually been to Andermatt already. In fact, I know it quite well.

We skied there a few times when I was a young soldier, and that was of course many moons ago. Very clean, very white, and, of course, very boring. But before we don the hiking gear and embark on our crusade of discovery, Madelyn, we need to grab Erica Vine. Please check that your passports are both in date and could you possibly ask Erica to bring her little red book along? She'll know what you mean."

Hastings stopped talking and stared back at her, then tried fusing the uneasy tension in the air. According to Hastings, every time he mentioned Erica's name, Madelyn would go into some sort of anti-female campaign and shrug her shoulders.

"And besides, you would look great in those ladies' Swiss national dress costumes—you know the ones—with the white. Your things . . . well, you know what I mean," he said out loud, almost alluding to the size of her buxom bosom. Then he stopped 'digging the hole' he had just created, and shot her a beaming wide smile.

"No, I don't know what you mean, Mr Hastings, and if you are implying, no, let me be more direct with you this time, are you saying my boobs are too big for this dress? And, that they would somehow really stick out in a tight fitting embroidered white criss-cross lattice bodice of lace and probably leather, and draw even more unwanted attention, if so, then I am insulted."

Hastings had turned a slight embarrassing red sort of colour. He then turned and made his way quickly back to the kitchen and filled the kettle with water.

"I'll tell you what, I'll call Erica myself." He retorted, and flicked the 'on' switch of the kettle. The Doctor smiled back and almost giggled after he had left the room.

Then she decided to have another pop at his ego. "I cannot imagine you in those tight leather hosen either, Mr Hastings. I think you should stick with your grey, boring tweed suit for now. Must be a certain nightmare in the winter with those leather schoolboy shorts anyway, don't you think? And, then again, we don't want to embarrass the complete Swiss national population either now, do we?" she responded, and then searched her clutch bag for some lip cream. Madelyn began applying the gloss to her soft, pink lips with her index finger then slouched lazily backwards, slowly falling deep into the soft covering of the Mexican sofa, thinking about her impending excursion to the Swiss Alps, but a bit unsure where the divine Miss Erica fitted in to the Hasting's equation.

As she lay backwards, she spied a pile of documents lying on top of the rustic wooden Mexican table. What caught her immediate attention was the red satchel that contained a myriad of documents and a few beige folders marked with SS type motifs. The satchel itself looked as if it had been 'through the wars' and displayed many signs of good use.

She leaned forward and pulled out a single piece of paper from within the file and scanned its detail. By her reckoning, there were approximately two thousand 'dead letter' boxes scattered across Europe. Well, two thousand boxes according to the paperwork she was reading and, that was two thousand places where potential books, ledgers trinkets or whatever, even relics, could have been secreted away out of sight by the many Knights of the Order over the past 200 years.

She placed the list back on the table and waited for Hastings to return with the coffee. Hastings returned to the living space with two warm, brandy laced coffees and sat at his desk. He then reached over and passed Madelyn her coffee cup. Then flicked open his laptop and started typing.

"I suppose I had better start the audit report. I think I should also start a journey journal, you know, like a book of places, points, people and whatever, things that turns up during the audit, things like those bloody coins, and receipts. Not sure if they will belong to the Order or not though."

Madelyn took a sip of her kaffee licqueur and took a single, deep breath then waved her right hand in the air and spouted out the word, "Whatever." Then took another long sip of her coffee and began playing with the gold booty at her disposal. Hastings, meanwhile, quizzed his scribbled notes and typed the opening statements to his new audit report:

Internal audit report—Ecosse Commandery.

Client: The Order of Saint John.

Dated: January, 2012.

Brief:

Auditor and author, Kemp Hastings of the Royal Lodge, assisted by Miss Madelyn Linn, biblical studies teacher, have trained their analytical lenses chiefly on the custodial processes of property handling whilst setting their intellectual sights toward the Order's internal procedures in general.

The approach to the 'book' and the actual audit report are recorded within the Agnus Dei, Knots and Krosses project, and is an attempt to loosely understand: a) the intellectual property at hand and b) the custodial common processes which are currently at work within the Order.

These simple, but highly effective systems, which are maintained by both the members of the Templar staff and the framework they adhere to, appear to be testament to how resilient man and process has been through the ages.

The outcome of the audit will comprise of an Audit Report & Journey Format.

Through the inquisitive process of due diligence coupled with an extensive literature review of an exacting level of detail, the author has discovered that the internal workings and common processes of such an establishment have never been fully explained to the academic community at large, or conversely, the establishment has never permitted documents, relics or other artefacts to be made public.

It is very unlikely that the Order will ever approve or grant permission for the establishment to be fully scrutinised under the scholastic or academic microscopes of society, and we must accept these conditions as such.

Rationale:

Since the advent of the Order, a certain amount of access was only granted to a select chosen few, chiefly because 'conclave' members have had their own sights trained on personal authorship and the eventual publication of their own interpretations of what the 'Templari Thesaurus' inventory may actually look like, but, personnel were somehow 'never' granted full access to the archives by the Grand Master or Grand Prior to the myriad of sensitive documents and artefacts held under the 'Order's remit as contemporary custodians.

It is, however, permissible to think that loyal and longer term members and scribes who exist within the Order did and do indeed, operate and maintain integrity regarding their own personal levels of both humility and honesty, common traits employed toward the preservation of this fantastic institution, whilst remaining beyond any chance of reproach. Thus, basically working together as an efficient, universal team of custodians harmonised under the premise of preservation and control for the Grand Master.

For the purposes of this audit the author raises the questions:

What has actually happened within the Order since 1812? And where are these so-called relics, documents and trinkets held? And, if they do exist, what items are hidden in the Templar vaults? And who are their custodians?

The copious amount of historical data, records and reports available would certainly indicate and confirm, that the 'Knights' Templar Order' have every God-given right to evolve in the manner that they do, especially in this volatile and politically unstable modern society, whilst chiefly operating under the most ultimate of secrecy—especially since the year 1307: a year which saw the potential demise of the complete Order under the tenure of the misguided French King, Phillip IV, 'Philip the Fair.'

CHAPTER FOUR

Knots

'Knot', definition: a small, tightly packed, group of people

'A knot of people were gathering', definition: a small cluster or huddled group

Events—24 hours earlier

The morning paper arrived on the doorstep of the old manse building. Hastings had heard the delivery boy clash the gate against the upright post as he had done repetitively now for so long; each morning sending a 'good morning' metal 'ching' across the wide farmyard area—something the boy seemed to do by default rather than malice. But it was a consistent wake-up call, nevertheless.

That moment in time which prompted the lazy, old, red rooster in the adjacent farm yard to spend a minute or two screeching and telling the world he was still alive by squawking out a few high pitched 'cock a doodle do's' to the world at large.

Hastings stirred, coughed twice, turned over, then fell out of bed in one motion. After which he grappled his way to his feet and eventually found the front door, that was of course having found the kettle first, he then picked up the local paper from the doormat.

He flicked open the tabloid pages as he walked back to the kitchen and read the main headline. It was then that he froze as the impact of the information hit his grey matter:

'Angus archivist found dead in suspicious circumstances'

The morning mail had also arrived as normal. Three letters were lying in no particular order on the coconut mat in the vestibule. Hastings smirked as he spied the words 'Welcome' that had been woven into the yellowy brown matting; a sentiment that Hastings would offer or extend only to a few inner circle or certain friends or special individuals he thought worthy of his invitation.

As he bent down to pick up the clutch of letters, the doorbell rang, and caused him to take a step backwards and quiz the shadow behind the frosted glass. He recognised a hat.

"Shit, not another parking citation, or council tax collectors bugging him into submission, in order to part with another twenty-eight pounds to clear his debt to society for water rates, or something else." He leaned forward and opened the door.

"Morning Guv'nor nice day for it . . . sign here, matey, please," requested the young DHL delivery man. Hastings barely acknowledged the delivery man's attire or his actual hat but signed the electronic 'thingy' with the magic electronic pen, then took the package and thanked the post person for his visit.

Hastings took the package and tossed it down on the Mexican coffee table top and headed to locate his coffee: he knew that it was either in the bathroom or in the lounge.

He took a deep breath and walked back past the table and glanced at the paper again, when a simple logo and address written in bold, blue lettering caught his attention. The package had been marked: From, Freddy, Restenneth.

Hastings knew that Restenneth was only a few miles away and would visit the Angus archives regularly, but never requested any ephemera or documentation to be sent to his home—no—that would be deemed quite lazy by his standards. It was much easier to drive the short distance and acquire what he was looking for; it was also an opportunity to chat to the staff, such as Freddy who was a wealth of local information.

Then the penny dropped. "Shit, the headlines, the archivist, the temple. Where was that strange death again?" he murmured, as he grabbed the daily rag, in order to read the article again, but this time, with deeper interest, only to realise that the recent death had only been his trusted researcher and contact within the establishment, Dr Rolf H. Toadie, or Freddy the Frog, to his friends, albeit he was of German descent.

The good, and late, Dr Toadie had on many occasions, over the past five years, furnished him with so much detail that often the Doctor would go well-beyond the call of council duty in order to assist Hastings in his many searches for answers.

Hastings huffed a little, then picked up the package. Then gripping the small white tab, he pulled it smoothly and began unzipping the paper seal of the package. He then flicked open the envelope and looked inside. To his surprise he found a medium sized booklet. He turned the envelope upside down and caught the book as it slipped out into his hands. He instantly recognised the Templar crest on the front cover.

"What the fu . . . is this all about then Freddy? What have you got yourself into this time my friend?"

He muttered away to himself, recognising the book as a medieval instruction manual on how to 'don armour', chiefly because it was written in large gothic lettering across the front cover, and of which, he was accustomed to viewing the older type Latin text through exposure to this particular ancient language during his many investigations.

The book was littered with incredible and highly detailed information in the preparedness for battle. And although the script was partially hand written it complimented the block text very neatly with a hand written set of instructions.

The flow of the lettering appeared to be in an older form of Latin or Deunos inscription, and was easily 14th century by his unprofessional reckoning.

He flicked slowly through the pages and absorbed the contents of the pamphlet. He took a drink of his warm coffee as he quizzed the pages, especially the little drawings by each paragraph that showed buckles, fastenings and pins that held the armour together.

That was when he noticed that some of the pages had somehow been fused together and showed signs that either a residue or a sticky, yellowy substance had managed to penetrate the pages and seal them together.

He opened the pages as smoothly as he could, flicking the pages over to leaf number 29 and then stopped. He picked at pages 30-34 and then flicked the corner of the smooth vellum. Then muttered away again to himself. "I know who could undo these pages professionally for me and without causing any damage and authenticate this little beauty at the same time."

He then flicked open his mobile phone with one hand and then tapped the speed dial 'number one' on the keypad as he walked around his apartment, and called his trusted new partner and 'document authenticating' lady and guru: Dr Madelyn Linn.

As he perused through the remaining pages of the book, he found a small yellow 'stick it' leaf note, which had been stuck to the back page of the document. It read:

> Hastings, you must get this book to the Fisher Kings, Dundee ASAP. The Black Lodge will stop at nothing to get hold of this book. Your life is already in peril if you do not act quickly. Bury away at all costs!

> See you in Himmel (Heaven), Freddy.

Madelyn was already close by to the village and a short distance from the little town hamlet of Brechin. She had been making her way to meet one of her journalist friends, and local newspaper reporter, Jennifer Crossgrave, who in her capacity as news correspondent had recently printed an article on metallurgy for the local press.

The feisty, female reporter was more than eager to hear more about the results of an earlier 12th century acquisition find that was discovered a few weeks prior. Madelyn had authenticated the accompanying manuscript of the sword and had dated it to the year 1187.

The Doctor, having spoken with Hastings, called Jennifer and made her excuses. Then arranged to meet with her later in the week. Then she headed straight for Hasting's modest abode, six miles away.

Having made herself fresh and presentable en route, but only thanks to the car's interior mirror, she eventually parked the Range Rover up alongside the garden curtain wall outside the manse and ambled toward the manse.

She located the doorbell to the Hastings' lodgings, whereupon she found that the door had been left open and she marched straight on in.

"Morning, Kemp. How is the hangover this morning?" she said, rather loudly, making her presence known and she walked straight into the small kitchen area and flicked the kettle switch to 'on'. "So what's the script this time? You mentioned a booklet on armour."

Hastings walked through from his study room and placed the parchment straight into her hands.

"Morning, Miss Linn. Yes, thank you. I am well too, thank you! How are you this fine day?" he said, very sarcastically. "Do you know how to unstick these gooey pages in the middle of my new book, please? I think it might be sticky coffee or sticky toffee pudding, or something," he said, flashing the sugar spoon across her eye line.

Madelyn searched her bag and found her glasses, placed them on her pert little nose, then quizzed the yellowish pamphlet. She took about forty seconds to quiz the vellum and made an instant conclusion. "Well, it's definitely 13th century, or even earlier and the writing is quite exquisite, and if you look at the symbology on these two pages here, and here, you can see the clear line of running script—very professional. It's not sticky coffee or pudding, Kemp, it's honey, bees' honey.

These pages have been deliberately fused together with good, old, gold, sticky 12th century honey. If you look here and here, there is a constant seam or a lighter coating or smooth application, and with two double blobs at the leading edges. Mind you, not normal practice for medieval times, I grant you, but definitely made by some 700 hundred year old honey bees. More coffee please, and no syrup."

Hastings picked up one of the coffee cups and stared back at her, then spoke. "An accident?"

Madelyn replied with clear, succinct authority in her tone of voice. "Oh, no, Kemp, no accident. This is quite deliberate. Have you got a scalpel or razor or something sharp? The book is old but if you look here . . . when you hold it up against the light you can clearly see the pages have been used as an envelope of sorts. There is something stuck within its folds too, can you see?"

Hastings was mystified, how could he miss so much detail in the thick pages. But, then again, it was a good night out with his chums last night, and he had no intention of investigating the biological product of bees let alone coupled with 12th century document appraisal and authentication, which was simply not on his morning's agenda.

He then headed off to the medical cupboard in the bathroom to find a scalpel and most likely another headache tablet.

"Here you go, young lady. This one I use for modelling, but it is still a scalpel. Sorry, I am all out of PM40's or any other post mortem examination tools."

Madelyn drew him another long, gloomy glare and he marched off to make another hotter coffee. Meanwhile, the Doctor cut a straight line across the top seam of page 32. Using the razor sharp scalpel, she cut the vellum with the precision of a heart surgeon at work, then gingerly removed the contents.

The thin page of yellow coloured vellum was very unique and had been folded three times and the word 'Thesaurus' was clearly written on the outer page. She unfolded the document and took a rather deep breath as she spied the writing on the primary panel.

"Oh my goodness!" she exclaimed, finding the soft comfort of the settee and sat down.

Hastings, meanwhile, sat down opposite her and smiled. "So what is it? A treasure map? A blank cheque from the Queen of Sheba?"

Madelyn nodded her head and reached over for her coffee. "Well, Kemp, that's exactly what it is, or it could be. It is a list of relics, people's names, and not just any people either, just a few ancient Knights' Templar type people. But, what is really exciting is the location of some ancient Templar vaults and coffers."

Hastings laughed out loudly. "Yeah right." Then shook his head from side to side. "Another fruitless treasure trail. The world is littered with this shit. I bet this is another one of those 'follow me and get rich medieval quick pyramid' schemes."

Madelyn shook her head from left to right and almost agreed, as he smirked, then took another sip of his drink. "Well, that might be true, Kemp, but this parchment is dated to at least two hundred and fifty years earlier than your book on medieval armour. This part of the vellum, here, is dated as June 1812. But, this portion here, no, that is easily 12th or 13th century.

The hand writing is totally different and is penned in early gothic, French style Latino with different ink. This list was been placed here deliberately, hidden away from prying eyes and I think not for general distribution either, or conversely, was misplaced here. Unless, again, it was deliberate. Do you know what 'St John, KT GM' means?" she asked, then turned the letter around and read off some more interesting detail, then read out loud what she could distinguish as writing. "It says on this parchment the words 'Order di Templari thesaurus'. That means that this could be an authentic inventory of the Order's wealth in the year 1812, and if you look here . . . it is clearly written 'Ecosse', and, Kemp, that means Scotland."

She smiled and took another drink of her coffee.

Hastings smirked and explained what the St John's Order was all about and what it actually meant, and that it was a continuance document of the Order's modern day existence, taken from what might have been the original 1127 game plan.

Hastings explained the details and touched on a few not-so-well-known phrases and acronyms held within the Order's extensive vocabulary.

"Madelyn, the GM clearly stands for the Grand Master, and KT, well, that's Knights' Templar. But to be marked down or written or even placed together on a single list is not unusual. But what is more of a concern to me is that the Order just does not telegraph its internal affairs. The establishment is just not that stupid. I mean these Knights were rather intelligent people; they constructed cathedrals, churches, excavations and fortresses, and commanded a naval fleet of vessels. Goodness, they even designed what we now know as the modern banking systems.

I think that if they, the Order, wanted this to be public knowledge, then they would have slapped it straight on the CNN mid-day news. Not wrap it up in a book to be locked away in a library for accidental discovery." He broke off and quizzed the internet on his laptop. Then he sent a couple of emails as Madelyn sipped more of her sweet, brandy laced coffee and watched as Hastings tapped away furiously at the 'qwerty' key pad.

"Kemp, you are aware that this could be an authentic treasure inventory list? And a document belonging to the actual Knights' Templar? And that there is probably only one of these actual lists in existence at any one time?" She stopped talking and waited for a response from her investigative partner who had stopped typing and had reached for his coffee cup.

The coffee cup had now managed to suspend itself between his upper and lower lips; the contents were waiting to be consumed. His brain was distracted and was busy, three hundred miles away searching for 'a why and a what', then he contemplated the 'what' more rigorously.

"And the 'what' was? Yes, what was the 'what'?" he asked himself. What has a book on medieval armour to do with Templar treasures? Let alone even suggest the whereabouts of any hidden riches, or any details even alluding to biblical booty.

The revelation had caught Hastings' direct attention and now the very interested and almost fanatical 'Biblical Investigator' was becoming excited and more than aware of a hidden world of esoterical mayhem that existed beyond the norms of society, a subject that consumed his desire for knowledge. A notion which sparked his desire to investigate the subject as far and deep as possible. Even if it meant digging up the Fuhrer himself.

As the couple discussed the new found list, Madelyn became aware of a car pulling up outside the clutch of buildings and had parked up beside her Range Rover, and the occupants of which were taking great interest in her machine.

"Kemp, we have visitors," she said, whilst stepping back from the window. Hastings sprang to attention and made his way to the window. He spied the red BMW being parked up a hundred yards or so away from his gateway.

"Okay, let's get out of here. That's the same car that was in Dundee and at the railway station yesterday, and the car mentioned in my last email from the Fisher Kings. The email said that I should endeavour to take extreme caution as there are ad hoc treasure seekers chasing gold coins from World War II."

Madelyn grabbed her coat and bag as Hastings thrust his laptop and the inventory list into his bag. He then pushed the two coin bags under the sofa. After another check, Hastings watched as the visitors were checking the names on the adjacent doors and were pointing over toward the manse.

The couple then opened the window to the rear of the building and climbed down the emergency fire escape ladder.

"I always park the Jaguar at back of the house," he said.

A few moments later, a red shadow quietly slipped out the farmyard courtyard and onto the main street then took off at great haste into the countryside.

"Do you think those morons are following us?" asked Madelyn, as she quizzed the view from the rear window of the car as it sped through the avenue of trees.

"Not for long," responded Hastings, and he squeezed the accelerator a little more.

CHAPTER FIVE

Krosses

Definition: saltire less commonly, saltier [ˈsɔːlˌtaɪə]

(History/Heraldry) Heraldry on crest—consisting of a diagonal cross on a shield

X marks the spot:

The Teutonic Order Palermo

After ensuring the coast was clear Hastings had returned to his home, and in the comfort of his abode he picked up the loose pieces of paper that sat neatly on top of his bedside cabinet, he had been meaning to read the contents at least three times over the last couple days but never somehow managed to find the time.

Starting to read the contents he wandered through his apartment as he did on occasions like this, only stopping now and again to negotiate a table or a doorway that he encountered. He smirked and tutted as the story he read began to unfold and was making a certain logic in his investigative world.

The year was 1170. The location was the Basilica of the Magione: a Norman styled church belonging to the Cistercian order of monks. The structure itself was located on the outskirts of the rural village of Palermo.

The assembled '**knot**' of clerics watched on, as the body of the most recently murdered cleric was dragged by horse and rider through the streets as a sign of change toward hostile aggression. A sign of the times as the Holy war raged through middle Europe and where the many churches were easy targets for the unscrupulous tyrants and vagabonds, legions of robbers who scourged the Earth and were systematically looting God's houses of their precious booty and there was no-one to protect the vulnerable clergy who sat within.

The holy war raged on for a further four years and eventually came to a resolve and certain stability returned to the lands. After a very historical and turbulent period in time, the Palermo church eventually was ceded to the Teutonic Order by King Henry VI von Hohenstaufen circa 1194-1197, where the Knights had established themselves as a working Sicilian Order.

The Teutonic Order ran business up until circa 1787, with such an affect that King Ferdinando of the two Sicily's decreed the basilica and cloister to be part of the royal demesne; a standing in society that brought exclusive patronage and established the Order firmly on the global map, which duly became a Sacred Military Commandery and was basically administered by the Prince of the Royal family.

The Palermo Order still functions today and holds many investitures throughout the course of the year. However, back in the days of January 1812, King Ferdinando of Naples and Sicily, and incidentally, Grand Master of the Order, was actually resident in Sicily during the Napoleonic era of destruction.

And had delegated powers of 'alter ego' and privileges to his son, Prince Francesco, should he, the King, be inexplicably murdered or maimed as a result of his unhealthy fascination towards war.

Hastings took another deep breath and ran a hand through his soft brown hair and spoke softly.

'Why the hell in God's name would you take an unhealthy interest in war?' he read on.

It was also at this time that early British influence began to infiltrate the Palermo Order and many great hunting expeditions were said to be had at the magnificent hunting lodge of Fizucca—an understanding of bonding and unprecedented cohesion of British Diplomats and their Military Generals.

The Order held many occasions for celebration but one celebration in particular was that of St George's day, and was celebrated with a bit more pomp and ceremony than usual, and was attended by The Knights' Templar Order—Europa, Ecosse.

Prince Francesco had received the fourth copy of the 'Templar Thesaurus' as an additional undertaking to ensure that the Italian Order and the local 'under order' or the Sicilian 'family' were in complete harmony, and forged complex relationships to ensure that the country's riches and ancient relics were always in safe hands.

'Well that makes total sense, so we have been doing the right thing'. He muttered then wandered off to take a shower.

CHAPTER SIX

Wehrmacht

The hustle and bustle of city life was very active as the BMW pulled up alongside the red Jaguar, just as Hastings placed his mobile phone back in the recess next to the CD panel. He noticed that the rear windows of the BMW had been blanked out, but just as the car slowly drew opposite, he smirked at the driver then spied three, small hi-tech VHF & HF antennae clearly visible on the roof.

He instantly wondered whether or not the car belonged to the police or the special branch, and almost began searching his pockets for his own driver's licence in case they wanted to be a pain in the proverbial rear end. Then suddenly, for some insane reason, he cast his mind back to three days prior, revisiting the events during his unscheduled visit with Madelyn to the office of the Fisher Kings, and again just yesterday at his home.

He tried to determine whether this was the same car or not. The windows were not blanked out the last time he spied the BMW. Then, just as the vehicle moved off, he spied the number plate; it was Italian which confirmed his suspicions.

"Arseholes, what the hell do these people want from me? I am sure these buggers have been haunting me for quite a while; obviously this is those so-called treasure seekers. But normally they are not hostile and quite approachable," he muttered to himself.

He parked up the XK 8 crimson beast, almost making contact with the pay ticket machine, just narrowly missing the money box with his bumper, and found what he thought was his resident parking spot in the local car park.

Whilst he was in the process of exiting the car, he was accosted by two larger sized gentlemen. Both men were clad in rather long, black Gestapo type overcoats, and who had approached him from behind, just as he had parked the jaguar, but he had failed to see them loitering at the rear of his machine. He stared at them both up and then down, then smiled.

The taller of the two tilted his head to one side, then in typical German dialogue, he spoke. "Guten tag, Herr Hastings. How are you today? Do you have a little time for us? We have some interesting news and information to share with you," asked the more outgoing of the Gestapo-clad pair.

Hastings nodded and stepped out, away from his car and leaving the vehicle unlocked in case he had to flee in haste. He was unaccustomed to being confronted away from the comfort zone of his surroundings.

"Mr Hastings, I am Bishop Andreas Salmen of the Teutonic Order of St Johann in Palermo, where 'Unsere Acht Punkt Kross' is our motif. But our local Kommanderie hails from the city of Koln, in the western side of Germany. We have been following you for quite some time now, and of course, I see you do not have the lovely 'Miss Gammay' or should I say the beautiful 'Miss Linn' with you today.

Our women of today, they are not a happy bunch are they? They always want to change something. If it is not their hair, it's their fingernails. It's all about their appearance, you know, they always want to look pretty and attract men. Too many changes all too often for my liking—don't you think?

I suppose they would eventually change their names, over time, especially when married." He then chuckled in a rehearsed sort of 'plastic' laughter. "I must simply apologise for our stalking of you like this, but we need to ensure that the government officials and the military of the British and Egyptian establishments are not following you. They can be such a pain, and they always seem to know where we are and you as well, of course.

We have observed them closely. You must have a GPS microchip fitted somewhere in your car? My colleague here is Colonel Rheinard Engel of the ancient Abwehr Order und Das Bundeswehr Archaeological Society, and, himself, a fellow monk of the Teutonic Order. The Colonel, and I, have been tasked to recover some rather interesting artefacts on behalf of the Palermo, Italian and German Orders' artefacts, which have 'disappeared' from our collective churches' clutches."

Hastings found himself caught up in a scene which, on the face of it, seemed rather funny, and thought back to a series on the telly where people just simply screwed up the German language wholesale, and he giggled inwardly as the leather-clad German rattled on.

"And we have discovered recently that your particular skills and research techniques could assist us and, of course, aid the Vatican to acquire such artefacts, and place them back in our Deutsche and Italian museums."

Hastings stood up and was somehow still feeling small in stature, pitched against the two rather larger German henchmen, and he moved backwards slightly as he spoke, whilst negotiating a quick exit strategy.

He then responded. "Okay, Herr Colonel, what is it, exactly, that you are after? As you already seem to know that I specialise in holy artefacts and you also know that I have a partner. Are you after any object in particular?" he asked, as he fumbled in his pockets, searching for his little black HMSO note book just as the officers stared at one another.

The Colonel smiled and looked directly at his colleague and nodded before speaking. "We are after about 200 million dollars of gold coins and bullion, Mr Hastings: our homeland treasures! Riches, which were torn from the clutches of the Wehrmacht in 1946/7. Although you will find that the Americans got most of the consignment, but, and a very big but, Mr Hastings, they appeared to have mislaid quite a substantial amount of it elsewhere," he paused, and stared upwards at the sky, then lowered his gaze. Then he drew Hastings an odd sort of angry, contemptuous grin, then continued reciting his account of what Hastings was desperate to hear.

The German continued, "And it is perhaps today, this gold bullion that sits in their big, secure Fort Knox vault in America, but, we know of some additional details, information that says not all of our Reichsbank gold was recovered from Bavaria. And some of our treasures, the treasures of our people, Mr Hastings, mainly gold, was sent into middle Europe and then onwards here into your Scotland. And, of course, you are Scottish, Mr Hastings, and you should have more of a fighting chance of success in helping us locate our wealth—certainly a far better chance than we will ever have. Of course, we will share the proceeds with you, and pay you handsomely. Or, at least, a healthy percentage of the haul—if you can help us locate our 'Heimland shatz?'"

The other, so-called monk, placed a finger over his lips, nodded, then muttered in broken English. "Genau, yes! Exactly, but we know that a British army gunner team acquired three trucks belonging to the Fuhrer early in May 1946 as well, and eventually slid out of Switzerland under a cloak of darkness and stealth, and moved the precious load by boat from, we think, somewhere near Genoa, taking with them a rather high percentage of our country's wealth. We are unsure of the actual dates but, we know this event took place in our history.

We also have located some credible documents that point us in the direction of the Swiss authorities—invoices, transaction documents from the Swiss bank to Himmler himself, indicating that the powers of the establishment within Europa hid the treasures away from their greedy Bundes Kanzler or Ministers' eyes. We think they have been in collusion for that past 70 years, and now it is time for reconciliation. And we are here to collect."

Hastings was bemused and entertained at the same time. Although he knew some snippets of information, he was not about to divulge his knowledge of what he had learned so far.

Hastings had made up his mind that these treasure seekers were indeed certifiable nutcases trying to find a booty that was otherwise not up for grabs. He would have to play the game with them and get these madmen on his side, that was if he was to continue with his more important task and audit without any further surprises.

The Officer then spoke up again. "We also have a copy of an old Nazi map and an older Templar inventory list dated for the year 1542, but it is of course no use to us at this time. It is useless without the actual deciphering code; a bit like our war time enigma machine our 'magic' machine, Mr Hastings. We need two important pieces of the jigsaw to make it work. But today we are far more advanced, we have sophisticated equipment to assist us, and we have scanned many locations. We know the Knights' Templar and our Teutonic Brotherhood are hiding Germany's wealth somewhere from our grasp, and that quite frankly, will simply not do.

They have records that point to your little Roslin Chapel. We think it might be just as simple to create a little distraction and perhaps blow the little chapel out of the ground and find the riches for ourselves.

You see we are aware that the Brotherhood of the German persuasion are systemically eroding away our belief systems from within our establishment, and have been, shall we say, removing some of our identity and selling it on to the highest bidders, and we just cannot allow that to happen either, Mr Hastings.

So, as a further example of our control, now that we are armed with our new acquired knowledge, we have discovered that your good Dr Toadie and colleague, who incidentally, had also been our contact in Scotland for nearly 15 years, had been somehow been involved with this despicable crime against our Fatherland and was handling artefacts in and out of Europa.

Although it was only recently that we learned that he had been physically involved in selling our relics and artefacts for substantial amounts of cash to the highest bidders, and of course, as you know, Mr Hastings, he is now dead."

Hastings was nodding as the German was conducting his spiel.

"Surely you don't intend to go destroying churches and chapels with explosives and weapons do you. That would go against all of the Order's ethos of preservation."

The German Officer dismissed his comments and continued burbling. "But please believe us, Mr Hastings, we don't normally kill our own kind either, although, we do think about ensuring loyalty but death is a bit extreme. But we believe the Americans found out that Dr Toadie was about to blow the whistle about the Toplizte Gold that he held in his possession, a revelation to the local press to save his skin.

That was before we arrived here and obviously we had arrived too late to save him. Perhaps your American transatlantic cousins are not all that friendly either. If I was to tell you that Doctor Toadie was a direct descendant of the Fuhrer himself, Mr Hastings, would you be surprised, and would you actually believe me? Well you can trust me when I say please, don't be surprised in any shape or form because he is, or was, He was the second son of three Grandsons from the Aryan race, it is rumoured that Adolf Hitler fathered more children than history will ever tell you, but das ist ein andere geshickte, an entirely different story indeed. Mr Hastings, on that little note, we shall say he, Dr Toadie, is no more, so? Will you help us or not, bitte, Herr Hastings?"

Hastings momentarily agreed to assist the pseudo Knights whilst working out an exit strategy should the need still arise. He thought again about the demeanour of these two raving lunatics who appeared 'not' to have a good solid understanding of how the mechanics of the order functioned, let alone their physical presence clad in two Wehrmacht trench coats, and more sadly how the English language was constructed. He smiled and got back into his car.

The German Army Colonel stood by watching as Hastings got back in his car and closed the door, he then slowly lowered the car window, in anticipation of not instantly fleeing from his newly found partners in 'criminal misgivings' who now appeared to be less violent than he had given them credit for.

After a few more minutes of loose discussion Hastings was furnished with a bright yellow Nokia mobile phone for contacting the not so 'Teutonic Order.'

A short time later he found himself sitting in the car park still quizzing the morning's events. He then called another telephone number provided to him by the Lieutenant Colonel Marquis, of the Atholl-Mar secret Army, and waited patiently for the Colonel to make his excuses and remove himself from a high ranking military meeting in order to talk with him.

"Colonel, I need a favour. I need to get a couple of fanatical lunatics off my trail until I finish my audit. Can you help me, please?"

CHAPTER SEVEN

Colonel Marquis of the Grand military order flicked open his laptop computer and trawled the electronic database and soon found a series of military written accounts pertaining to World War II active service.

He located a specific service account and displayed the document on to the large projector screen as his assembled audience waited in anticipation to learn about war tactics. In fine military tradition the Officer stood at the podium and stared aimlessly for twenty seconds before speaking, he wanted to create an awkward silence before he began his lesson.

'Gentlemen, this is of course highly secret information and if you are caught divulging any of it's contents to any living soul then we will have to pull out your liver and spleens and give them to the Quartermaster in order to make lunch'

There was a hum of laughter and the audience settled.

'Anyway, moving swiftly on, the date was the 6th **June 1943**—'**Operation Avalon**' was hatched, and incidentally the 6th of June is just a coincidence and no relevance to 'D-Day'.

The Colonel flicked the power point display to reveal the header banner onto the huge white panel in front of him and to his clutch of new assembled 'Rodneys' for learning purposes, it read:

British Gunners Mobilise

He then started to recite his lesson for the day.

'The German command post's heavy walled canvas tent had been pitched and established, and was open for wartime business. The tent sat a few hundred meters off into the far right of the sparse forest and semi-submerged in the undergrowth. The tent itself was deliberately placed spitting distance from where the two tracks merged into a single route through several rows of fir trees that dominated the surrounding area.'

The Colonel started to engage each member of the assembled audience with direct eye contact as he spoke, whilst simultaneously waving his arms in elegant gestures trying to place a certain emphasis on his lesson. He continued for several minutes.

'To the far east of the copse another single mountain pathway ran through the middle of the thicker treeline and rugged terrain and eventually disappeared through an abundance of conifers in the Bavarian forest of the Bergwald, and stretched int almost darkness.

The forest itself was situated near to the village (Ort) of Bischofshofen: a small rural clutch of houses sitting almost in obscurity approximately, forty-four kilometres south east of Hitler's mountain fortress: 'The Eagle's Nest'.

Sitting rather picturesque, below 'The Eagle's Nest' is the somewhat larger town of Berchesgaden a town which maintains an important arterial roadway leading North into Southern Germany, where the 'bahn' or road was heavily defended by the Wehrmacht troops in their efforts to support SS Troop movements.

Which was in itself a certain logistics nightmare for the enormous task of relocating heavy and light military hardware across the Region, critical equipment that was destined for the Russian border lines in support of the on-going efforts of War torn Germany of 1944, and was quite literally fully engaged in the art of political genocide.

Although Germany was busy mobilising its War assets toward a new target location nearer toward the Russian front, it had not lost its focus on world domination and was harvesting what riches it could acquire in its progress.

The logistics themselves was a fairly complicated task and a certain mind meld for the Heer Officers to execute their complicated plans as they moved four hundred tanks and twenty one thousand troops at a few days' notice in order to face the onslaught of the cold Eastern Bloc countries.'

The lesson plan was going very well as the Colonel flashed a series of photographs across the screen to keep his captured audience interested.

'At work during this time was a complex framework of people and a system of control that was diligently being applied, not only for moving tanks, people, guns and rockets and other hardware, but was also the same mechanism employed to move vast amounts of sensitive ancient, religious or valuable objects acquired by the Wehrmacht's forward line assault troops in the same safe manner.

A concerted strategy of pillage and acquisition as the German Army moved through middle Europe, each new ambush plundering museums, houses, castles and many bank vaults in their undying efforts to appease their tyrant leader and their many gold seeking greedy Generals in the process.

Hitler, at this time, had his sights firmly set on Paris and the plethora of expensive art work completed by the great many masters that were to be his just for the having, either to be stolen or relieved from their current owners under the Fuhrer's volatile and murderous tenure of control.

The complex and often complicated process of war logistics was not only at work for warring hardware and heavy machine being chiefly managed by an 'Inner Order of subordinates'—a team who were 'running silently' in the background and of which were sympathetic to the Teutonic Order of religious Knights.

And, who ironically were the same clutch of subordinates that were working and moving mountains in order to procure and move the more obscure of military acquisitions which were in the form of yachts, aircraft and expensive vehicles along with holy relic's, riches and trinkets of Christendom, and other global icons that had changed the face of mankind.

These local spoils of war were secured in the various vaults of the Berchesgaden Funksturm Kaserne and were recorded as being sent deep underground to be stored in chambers that sat almost one hundred and twenty feet below ground level. Other locations included copper mines at Kaiseroda and other unused coal shafts.

The movement of which was controlled under the watchful eye of the Wehrmacht's or SS General's, who were often at odds with the Fuhrer's management team as the high ranking officials began laying claim to specific artefacts, and, if the many wartime rumours were to be believed the Generals were getting very greedy indeed.

The asset management team were given specific areas of time and history to target and were procuring items that fitted into that specific era or time slot. Eventually the teams had been tasked to split up this great mass of wealth and the spoils of War in order to keep them segmented under a blanket of secrecy, and details of which were only known to the select chosen few.'

The audience was mesmerised as the seasoned veteran continued to keep them amused.

'Sadly gentlemen, in the fullness of the Holocaust warring time, it was not uncommon to find 'German casualties of commerce' lying alongside the innocent dead war victims, as the SS cleaned up their many acts of deception and deceit, and had on occasions murdered their own kind in order to hide the wealth, or simply to eradicate any evidence trail of their activities, or conversely, deal with the potential of being double crossed by those who had served them in the first place.

One of the primary controlling Officers of the War booty was the Nazi Interior Foreign Minister who had other interests at heart, especially, interests that lay in the realms of his own preservation and one who was busy hatching his own master plan.

He was busy executing a strategy that was to see him and his family safe, secure and wealthy in the not too distant future and had planned to defect once his wartime 'portion' was safe on foreign soil; Hungary was becoming a likely location to resettle.

Whereupon, the Minister had set up a team of chosen specialists who were busy filtering acquisitions to a second secret location near to the body of water known locally as Lake Toplitz, a small sized, but very deep inlet loch in the middle of Bavaria.

The Nazi interior foreign Minister incidentally was also the owner of a small mountain villa building known as Schloss Fuschel or Castle Fuschl which served his purposes very well as the Villa lay in close proximity to 'the Eagle's Nest' in Berchesgaden, but situated far enough away from the immediate and inquisitive prying eyes of the SS Generals and the Wehrmacht.

The castle was located some forty six kilometres to the north of Berchesgaden, sitting neatly within a tranquil forest setting of greenery and foliage and secluded from view of any external agencies.

It was at Schloss Fuschel near to the House of Joachim, (von Ribbentrop) that nine German soldiers were busy loading three Bundeswehr Mercedes flatbed trucks with what appeared to be a series of converted heavy duty ammunition boxes.

Each ammunition cell was two foot wide and four foot in length, and had been clearly labelled with the unusual markings of the older style swastika and an odd 'Templar Kross' based on the Teutonic Order of the ancient world.'

The Colonel stopped his presentation and flashed a few more photographs of cargo boxes and documents that had been presented at the Nuremberg trials, then continued.

'The markings on each case were complimented by a neatly stamped stencil that ran along the external leading edge of the box and displayed the word 'Geheim' in bold red lettering.

The Colonel stopped talking and clapped his hands loudly making his audience shuffle in their seats. Fifteen Captains and Lieutenants of the Royal Artillery were being educated on the past exploits of their fellow Soldiers and Officers.

'The 36 boxes were fitted with steel studded, heavy duty padlocks and overlapping locking braces and clamps and each unit was embossed with the seal of the SS.

The skull or Totenkopf insignia was clearly visible and had been stamped into the actual moulding of the trunks. Another anomaly of this consignment was the presence of a red seal that was covering the key hole of each lock as it hung downwards on the flattened sides as attachments to the metal chest, forming a solid lid lock or retainer.

The boxes were eventually stacked two high then loaded onto the back of the trucks and were made ready for transit. It could be observed that each vehicle was furnished with an armed guard, and each driver was issued with a simple hand written sketch of a road map of where to go.

No words were written on the paperwork—they had been given just a series of odd ciphers and markers with instructions of when to stop and wait or where to extinguish the vehicle lights during any convoy routines.

Each flatbed truck had been fitted with a green overhead canopy to protect the undisclosed cargo and was tied down at the front and back. A part of the rear canvas flap had a cut out hole one foot in length with a smaller flap that hung loose, which was designed to accommodate the barrel of a single heavy 'MG 34' machine gun.

The truck in general for whatever purpose it was intended for, was clad in a more than average defence configuration with extra side plates of steel which had been added to the longitudinal panels of the flatbed and fitted for more than mere GS or General Service Cargo deployment.

The Feld Webel and the operations Field Officer took a final look into the last two remaining chests and agreed their contents of which was recorded as $10,000 face value gold coins and a series of gold amulets and necklaces that could easily have dated back to the 12th century or earlier.

The Feld Webel signed the financial ledger and placed it amongst several other pieces of paper, first having the accompanying Officer counter sign the sheet. He had then stuffed the ledger into the red, leather satchel which lay on the bumper tray of the Mercedes flatbed, then gave the Officer a set of thirty-six, large keys for safety.'

Another new screen flashed up the wording Field Deployment flashed twice then settled on a single screenshot of a large World War II deployment map. The Colonel was by this stage getting rather excited as he recited this account for the umpteenth time over the past year.

'Less than thirty clicks away, the British Army Gunnery Bombardier, 'Fred' Lewis, had just tuned the C41/C42 radio tuning unit into a set frequency, when a single spark arced from across the earth bond wire to the metal antenna base casing and the metal surface of the vehicle's bumper, a place on the vehicle where the external antenna was fitted, thus, described—as being 'state of the art'—1943, British Army radio system.

The Bombardier had been busy tweaking the two rotating knobs on the facia panel at the time of the spark as he was trying to tune the equipment and gain maximum radio signal deflection swing, when the infernal thing flashed up with an electric shock pulse throwing him almost ten feet backwards onto the soft greenery.

Meanwhile, his fertile military mind had been simultaneously constructing a message in his best German language in order for his team to send a series of crypto messages across the German side of the Ethernet, and he had been momentarily distracted by the electric shock.'

The military Officer pointed his finger in the air and stood next to a young subaltern.

'A warning gentlemen in for you wish to play with electricity, in the report we find that the Bombardier had recorded his exploits that day in the Signals log book the 'F-Sigs 266.'

He lay back on the grass and had laughed inwards to himself, then picked his sorry arse off the damp ground whilst checking his fingers to see if they were all still present and correct on his left hand. But more importantly.

The message he was busy concocting was a deliberate fabrication of great detail. It would be created in the form of a half-cocked, encrypted electronic bundle message designed to confuse the enemy at large—the team, knowing full well that all radio signals would be rigorously interrogated by the Abwehr radiotelephony and counter measures intelligence group. The message itself was eventually written down by the Bombardier and read by Lance Bombardier Robert Thornett, or 'Bobby T' to his peers, where he, in his capacity as CP signaller, fitted the highly secret 'circular data' punch card into the radio facia panel then closed the data encrypting device, prior to transmitting the 'not so very secret message' on the C41/C42 Larkspur radio to the German hierarchy.

The communications system had been previously harnessed into the military Quad vehicle and every effort was made to ensure that the truck would not suffer simple battery failure whilst in operation and, therefore, two banks of 12 volt lead acid batteries had been fitted and were complimented with a hand 'crank' generator for emergency purposes, a fitting that Fred had discovered was quite potent.

The 'Quad' as it was commonly known, was named after it's installation into the Royal Artillery in early 1943 and was primarily employed as a tow tractor vehicle to pull a single 25 pound field gun, Howitzer and ammunition trailer. The attachment of which sat rather conveniently in the middle of the tractor and gun units.

Of course, for this secret (Geheim) mission, the gun and ammo units had been left back on the safe side of 'no man's' land—a few hundred kilometres north, for very good reason.

To man and drive this pseudo German vehicle deep into enemy territory, a group of highly skilled specialists was recruited and after a comprehensive selection process a team was prepared.

The crew had also painted their Morris—(Quad) Commercial Artillery Truck with painstakingly careful detail in order to make the vehicle look as identical as possible to other vehicles in the fleet that the Wehrmacht maintained.

It was by paying very careful attention to simple detail by the gun crew that they had literally transformed the once British Artillery Quad vehicle into a pseudo German Army, armoured version of the Steyr 270 kfg—kraftfahrzeug

The truck itself was known affectionately by the crew as the 'FAT Bastard' and was painted with the Bundeswehr's current 1944 camouflage colour scheme. The team had removed all numbers and badges that would otherwise reveal the identity as to their vehicle's origins and also had the vehicle stencilled with an SS Swastika logo on each door with one larger decal on the larger roof panel.'

Another photograph flashed across the screen.

'The paint work was conducted in an attempt to thwart or deter any ariel attacks from the over enthusiastic ME109—Messerschmitt or Stuka pilots that roamed the valleys of the borderlands. And it was just after a few short weeks and the Quad appeared to be more German than its counterpart the actual German Steyr 270(a).

The team conducted some very basic driver training, after which they were introduced to the finished FAT Bastard 'Quad' in final preparation for their mission and embarked to the land of Jagermeister and mayonnaise.

Of course, in time honoured tradition, the team, having been served with secret orders and many counter intelligence briefings from their serving C.O.—Commanding Officer of the day—Lt Col Chris Stuart Nash R.A, and a few beers 'Blighty side', the crew were ready to embark on their secret mission.

The Colonel and Commanding Officer, for reasons only known to themselves, had nicknamed his part of the operation as 'Knots and Krosses', and after four days of final preparation and the issue of identity documents was complete, project 'Avalon'—Knots and Krosses—was a reality.

First Parade.

Sitting at the driving controls of the 1942 C8 'Quad' vehicle was driver, Gunner Gary Mills, who had aptly named the truck 'FAT Bastard' after his comparison toward his gun line, Section Commander's physical stature.

His Master and Commander being one soldier who did not venture toward the gymnasium too often. And of which, complimented the actual bulbous shape, design and technical name for the truck as the Field Artillery Truck (FAT).

Gunner Mills had been commenting on his JNCO's more substantial gut proportions on more than one occasion and loose comments which got the young Gunner several unsolicited slaps on the back of his ginger Geordie head, mainly for his cheek and out spoken views.

The full crew of this elite Artillery contingent, on the other hand, consisted of a further six volunteers who all spoke the German language at above colloquial level and had each been provided with additional skillsets to ensure that the mission was both successful and could be conducted with limited or no casualties.

Having completed their comprehensive training program consisting of weapon skills familiarisation with the MG 34 and pistols followed by Radio Telephony skills, they finalised with intelligence and information gathering techniques.

The crew was then introduced to two intelligence Officers—British Army Major Sam Caughey and Wehrmacht Offizier, Major Karl Heinz Goldstein, and who appeared to have blended quite well in the run up to deployment, albeit, the team remained somewhat negative about the cut of their new German uniforms which had been hastily tailored as a last minute measure

After final action and preparation, the team began their journey and were slipping over the German, Bavarian border, making their way to the heart of the Fatherland's Leadership cell which was 'The Eagle's Nest'.

The British Army Gunners had set up their listening station in the silence of night and were interrogating the German communications network in order to trace the whereabouts of any 'ad hoc' smaller non-routine convoy movements.

Or conversely, monitoring vehicle movements particularly South of Berchesgaden, in order to try and detect any communications or mentions of the illusive 'Templari Thesaurus' documentation. Documents that the British and American 'Establishment' knew existed, but had no real idea of their actual whereabouts.

After two weeks of stealthy deployment under the guise of an Abwehr Nazi communications listening post, the team eventually got their first break in the form of a singular ad hoc telecommunications message.

The signal intercept was dated as 14th June 27th, 04:24 hours, and a single transmission had mentioned a series of books and several library packages that had been found as part of a recent trawl by the German troops nearer to the Swiss border.

The German attack group had apparently ransacked a small chapel near to the southern Swiss border, and that was when the first mention of the 'Thesaurus' came to light as the words 'TEMPLARI' echoed twice in the headset of the signaller, which buzzed and crackled with a series of numbers: elf, drei, vier und dreizig . . .

The Colonel then sat on the edge of the desk and clasped his hands.

'Okay now we will park up the 'political' detail aside, and I will tell you the real story from my perspective having recited this particular ditty more than once. Gunner Bob Bedford was on shift as Signaller when the C42 crackled another series of numbers which hit his earshot through the Bakelite headset, only this time a lot clearer than normal. He feverishly grabbed his pen, knocking over his coffee in the process, just as the Larkspur radio system had started humming away merrily in the background. To his surprise, the transmission was repeated and the detail of which fell neatly into place, quite sensibly.

Gunner Bedford listened intently then hastily scribbled down the numbers and some other additional notes. After about forty seconds, he read his message back to himself and deciphered what he thought he had heard. He then compared the translation against the German crypto codex system, 'Klaar' designed by the Abwehr, then quickly left the command post to locate Bombardier 'Fred' and Major Sam.

Soon after the radio message was authenticated more than once, the complete crew were summoned into the tented CP (Command Post), and given a new set of executive orders. The Bombardier sat on the edge of the CP table and engaged the team.

"Right, listen up guys: we have located what we think is where one of the flatbed trucks may be or is actually located. Then he pointed to the small map on the pin board. Bob (Snoz) has done a great job and managed to intercept what we think are a couple of eight figure, map grid references which point to a castle, not too far away. About 36 clicks to the north of here.

Now, listen up guys, we are looking for a set of books, not gold, not diamonds, not artwork, and I know what you are thinking, why the hell am I risking my neck and arse for a couple of books, well, here's the deal, these books or inventories they are worth a zillion dollars and our glorious leaders, bless their little cotton socks want them back before anyone else gets their greasy mitts on them, it is as simple as that, so what we do is this: firstly, we locate the truck or trucks; secondly, we then observe where they are stowing the cargo, it could be an outhouse or could be in an annex building, this is important in case we need to conduct an ariel attack if we are not successful here, and, thirdly, we must have a few close up pictures—Tony!" said the Bombardier, pointing to Lance Bombardier Tony Perry who had a penchant for technical photography and had the most up-to-date Box Brownie camera, complete with carrying case, that the British Army could muster.

"We need photos of the people, and any other relevant detail." The Bombardier then ran his hand around his face mimicking 'mug shots'. "You need to get as close as you can, Tony, and if the opportunity presents itself and only if you can drive the trucks away then we do it! But, and I mean but! Only if we can do it SAS style."

Fred stood up and stared at Major Sam Caughey who stood in the doorway, nodding away like a plastic, fuzzy dog sitting on the back parcel shelf of a Ford Escort in agreement. His hand rolled, German cigarette almost burnt to a cinder as he thought about how he was going to move his command post quickly. Then, the Bombardier coughed a bit and sat down again on the CP table top.

"When we get the pictures, we bug out! Millsy (Geordie), pedal to the metal and don't spare the horses, keep heading deep south into Switzerland, don't stop until you fall off the end of a cliff and land into the sea, somewhere near Italy. As I have already said, guys, if we can grab a few trinkets then that's fine, but not at the expense of the exercise. We can grab what we can in the initial 'melee' that ensues, but it is so important that we try not to attract too much unwarranted attention to ourselves and, gentlemen when we get to Genoa then we can relax, but not until then. And remember, Gentlemen, we are deep behind enemy lines—probably deeper than most SS officers. Shit! That reminds me: radios. Bob, remember to send the blanket high pitch white spike signal channel before our assault that should distort any outgoing radio signals."

Major Sam Caughey then stepped forward and flipped back the tent panel then spoke. "Millsy, in case you are wondering that's south downwards on the map—in case you are confused, and please don't start walking or driving north once we 'bugout'."

The crew shared a subtle moment of laughter, then Fred added a few other pointers.'

As the Colonel stood up he was astounded to find that each man in the room had been completely engrossed in his tale telling and appeared eager for more.

"Now, finally Gunner Banner (Trotters) you are to don your full Major's uniform and sit up front in the cab with Major Sam and Gunner Mills, just in case we get rumbled, your German is far better than ours and you certainly have that Officer flair about you. And finally, gentlemen, we will meet up with Major Goldstein at some point nearer the Swiss border, any questions?"

he asked, then started tapping 'Trotters' on the shoulders. "And keep yer bloody hat on. It's so important to keep up the pretence as far as we can. The Krouts will have binoculars and radios, and if we are lucky they will spot the swastikas on the truck and our SS uniforms well in advance of any control posts, and hopefully will leave us alone."

By the 16th April 1944 a red, leather satchel and a well-used Box Brownie camera sat on the desk of Lt Col Chris Stuart-Nash R.A. in his new office, situated within the nice shiny new MOD offices, Whitehall, London.

The Gunner team had executed their task with overwhelming results and had got back to Blighty in time for tea and medals. They had acquired some excellent photographs of the castle and the people in and around it, specifically photographs of the 36 war chests that contained so much wealth, and were somehow also furnished not just with detailed photographs and information but, had also acquired a reasonable amount of gold treasures aptly named, 'Reichsbank gold'.

A massive haul of gold deposits and trinkets that now required the attentions of the British Military intelligence support group, and now had to somehow construct a plausible explanation as to how this $150,000,000 of Deutsche wealth came to land in the United Kingdom under the tenure of the incumbent Grand Master, Edward James, 10th Earl of Elgin and Kincardine.

During their concerted efforts of relieving the Wehrmacht of three flatbed lorries and a motor bike, the team all arrived back in Blighty, fourteen days after their initial assault on Schloss Feuchsl which had been implemented with great painstaking detail and obviously had paid off handsomely.

There was, of course, no casualties nor any gunfire, just an unhealthy amount of contaminated white spirits and a mixed bag of melatonin alcohol mixed concoctions that had somehow got into the water supply and bottles of wine within the castle's vaults, sending almost the complete inhabitants of the castle into a drunken, sleepy stupor.

The Command Post of the joint Allied Forces Commander, Europe, meanwhile had arranged a near border assault and an off chance Artillery barrage, in the pretext of distracting the German leadership to concentrate their efforts regarding their more northern operations, as the 'away team' waited patiently to mobilise out of the country.

Once en-route, the team were assisted, of course, by the Genoese underground movement, who had arranged a flotilla of large boats to move their precious cargo at very short notice.

The Genoese (Palermo) Order of the Temple had come up trumps and had acquired three suitably sized flat bottom vessels within twelve hours, whereupon, the transit of the wealth was simply cross loaded whilst still remaining in their original storage boxes—containers that we can or should be able to observe today if they exist.

For the Gunner crew, it was both victorious and sad at the same time, positive in the facts as the team gained a 'mission complete' on their many war service records, but, sadly because they had left one bastardised Royal Artillery C8 Chevrolet (FAT) bastard truck at the bottom of Lake Toplitz, Austria, and had somehow recovered thirty-six large ammo boxes, that were never fully accounted for. Or were they?

When questioned about the project 'Avalon.' outcomes by the wartime press, Lord Whatshisface of the Ministry of Defence declared that any booty brought into Europe via Switzerland was fair treasure trove, and then publicly condemned the Nazi regime for stealing it in the first place, then discredited any knowledge of such a ludicrous endeavour that was reported to have been executed so deep behind the highly embarrassing German lines.

After the war had ended nearer the latter part of 1945, and after a certain stability fell upon the border lands of Germany and Bavaria, a strike team was assembled to locate the actual salt mine of Kaiseroda and take possession of whatever artefacts were stored within the miles of underground tunnels. Sadly, this was where the Nazi machine had secreted their ill-gotten gains from the few concentration camps and locations from across Poland.

The release of such a find to the world's press resulted in world condemnation toward the Nazi war machine and was dubbed the Merkers' treasure. Later that year Lt Col Chris Stuart Nash Royal. Artillery received a healthy pension and retired from service with three bars and five war medals. But sadly never informed anyone about the actual meaning of the name of the operation, less for one person and that person was his boss: The Earl of Kincardine.'

As the Officer ended his lesson, a single screen was flashed up depicting the way to fond the new Officer's club.

CHAPTER EIGHT

✠ *Hugues De Payens—* ✠
Grand Master

Kemp Hastings picked up a small piece of paper that was tucked neatly at the rear pages of the booklet and read a short passage that had been written in early gothic calligraphy.

The script itself had been centrally placed and appeared to have been updated along its timeline and fortunately for Hastings, signed at the bottom by: HdP—GM KT. Al Aqsa, he read the content then flashed up his computer. As far as he was concerned this document was his authority to reach his goal in achieving a quality appraisal on behalf of his client.

Grand Priory
'Templari Thesaurus'

"There is an action and understanding, that should be undertaken by all Grand Masters and that action is as follows: 'The non-public 'Thesaurus Inventory' belonging to the—Holy Knights' Templar Order—will undoubtedly spend the remainder of its clandestine existence under a veiled shadow of secrecy, and most likely be held under lock and key for all time—secreted in an ecclesiastical system of vaults throughout Christendom. This process must continue without disruption or misdirection from any external influences.

HdP—GM KT

Succession Order Number: forty two (42). Chev Andrew Ramsay GM.—I have secreted this day the 16th *of October, 1695, 'Thesaurus' at Scone Palace and have assigned custody of new 'Thesaurus' to:*

- *Charles Edward Stuart—GM—Ecosse, Greyfriars, Edinburgh. CES-KT. Dated: 13*[th] *October, 1740.*

CHAPTER NINE

The Churchyard—Line of Roses

Hastings read the passage at least three times before he found himself actually acknowledging being caught up in the history of Templar succession Orders, and quizzed the document again with both respect and apprehension. He was wrapped up in the moment and found a quieter corner of the churchyard then sat down out of sight of any unwanted onlookers.

"Templari Thesaurus, is it that simple? That the Order just referred to the inventory list in its Latin translation, and not Magisterial or Order—now that was clever," he muttered softly, and smiled at the simplicity of the document's name. Scholars, globally, would be searching for a document with a far more complicated name for identification purposes or would be searching many documents that alluded to temple wealth that would be adorned with colourful crests, logos and other higher Order identification marks and signatures.

But Hastings was convinced that the less simpler detail would trip up the many scholars and lead them off to nowheres-ville, searching for some clandestine Templar records.

He was quietly contemplating what to do next and how he was going to find the correct authority to hand over the secret 'Inventory List' to, but struggled with his thoughts as to how he could facilitate its return without raising suspicions, and more importantly without becoming a casualty in this trail of greed and succession.

He heard a feint buzzing or purring sound somewhere off to the right of his earshot. Then gazed up for a split second, just as a low flying Lynx helicopter buzzed immediately overhead. The flying machine flew no more than sixty feet above the ground and was flying at least a hundred and twenty knots an hour as the high pitch tone of the multi-formed Kevlar rotors cut and sliced through the Scottish air.

The pilot was obviously joy riding and tree hopping in the process, narrowly missing the higher branches of the tree tops where the potential for the long landing skids of the chopper to easily get caught and fowl up on the taller foliage, bringing the chopper to a rather quick and tragic end of its joyous flight.

Hastings momentarily sprung back to reality as the chopper flew overhead and disturbed his immediate train of thought.

"Shit, he was flying very low," he said softly to himself whilst fighting back the urge to call his partner Madelyn Linn, just as the murmur of the Gems II turbines became a buzzing echo in the far distance. He decided otherwise and found her cell phone number and after a few seconds of ringing there was still no answer. He then tried her home number.

"C'mon, Maddy, where the hell are you, pick up."

Meanwhile, six miles away, the Army Air Corps battle configured Lynx attack helicopter had landed in a small copse next to a small church and had shut down both engines, whereupon, the pilot sat patiently waiting for further orders from—G-Ops—HQ MODUK or from the Earl of Mar's control centre.

The helicopter Commander then dismounted the aircraft and wandered a few feet from his transport still poised patiently for his iPhone to flash an approval text from his Commander in Chief.

It was not long before an incoming text caught his eye and earshot, requesting that he take a jaunt northwards and search for the red Jaguar car belonging to Kemp Hastings.

The pilot summoned the P2—2nd pilot and the helicopter was soon airborne again, heading back the way it had just flown, but flying much slower and more deliberate. Hastings, meanwhile, had got back into his car and was heading to another small church a few miles away.

As he negotiated the leafy lanes, Hastings took another glance at the red, leather satchel that sat on the passenger seat of the car and thought about how many people had actually held this sensitive Templar artifact in their possession and, if anyone apart from De Payens or other Grand Masters actually understood its significance.

After all, it was not easy to grasp the full range of The Knights' Templar inventory comprising of lands, palaces, churches, fortresses, vessels, documents and gold that easily stemmed into millions upon millions of pounds sterling.

Hastings sped beyond the boundaries of a long field of rapeseed that led into the village and was immediately alerted by the presence of the red BMW with the Italian number plates—the very same car belonging to the Teutonic Lodge as it passed him by travelling in the opposite direction at great haste.

He quizzed his rear view mirror and watched as the Beemer's brake lights suddenly flashed on and the car began slowing down. He increased pressure on the accelerator and floored the XK and was hitting almost 70 miles per hour and decided to pass straight by the church he was intending to visit, and decided that he would remain distant until it was safe to return to the otherwise quiet village of Lundie.

Hovering 100 feet above the single track roadway, the AH1 Air Corps Lynx pilot was maneuvering his aircraft into a more strategic position prior to executing a controlled hard landing on the tarmac below.

The pilot observed the BMW turn in the nearby layby 900 meters away, and it was then that he interrogated his IHADSS—Integrated Helmet Display Systems—for target acquisition. He had targeted the car first, then spoke into the small rubber microphone.

"Hello, Zero Alpha (OA) this is Mike Whiskey four two Charlie, (MW42C). I have observed two target vehicles, a BMW and a Jaguar, send mission requests for serial, one niner, over!"

The pilot's headphones crackled loudly, pitched against the hitch pitch whir of the Gems II power train, the turbine humming away at 80% of the power source as the aircraft's turbine kept the machine sitting in the hover as the power house resonated loudly in the background, when a voice broke the pressured silence in the Pilot's left ear piece.

"Hello, Mike Whiskey four two Charlie, this is Zero Alpha, execute eagle VCP—Vehicle Check Point on BMW detain or restrain as applicable, use of lethal force approved if fired upon, detail seven minute . . . over!"

The pilot acknowledged the message, then began nodding and gazed at his P2 assistant who was twiddling the little black switches on the Marconi AFCS interface, then pointed downwards towards the roadway below.

Within less than 20 seconds, the Lynx chopper had landed slap bang in the middle of the grey, tarmac road and touched down on terra firma just before the BMW had come into view.

The unsuspecting car driver barely having time to contemplate any evasive action and had rammed on the vehicles brakes, bringing the car to an abrupt halt, hard up against the muddy grassy verge.

The second pilot rapidly exited the air craft and had pulled out a loaded standard military 9mm, Browning hand held pistol from his hip holster and pointed the weapon directly at the passenger in the car.

He then spurted out a few commands in both German and English; commands that alerted the two occupants of the car that this was a well-controlled and orchestrated hit.

"Out and down on the ground. Hands over your head. That's both of you!" he shouted, with command authority.

"Quickly! And bloody schnell, schnell!"

He shouted again, just as the second occupant lay face down on the tarmac's surface. The pilot began burbling more information onto his audio system when he noticed an odd piece of paper sticking out of the pocket of one of his detainees; he leaned over and removed the vellum.

The man on the ground was about to say something or was about to move when the Officer cocked the nine millimeter and stepped nearer. '

"It's not worth the effort my friend, we are not quite ready to kill you chaps just yet, but be warned, we are watching you very carefully, your so called Priory and their ill intentions are not welcome nor wanted".

The Officer placed the parchment in his leg map pocket and stepped backwards. The document contained the following information and was written on a 1944—SS radio communications transmittal letter. The communication document had been embossed with logo of the imperial 3rd Reich.

Anfang: start

"Gestapo Offizier, Klaus Barbie Lyons, currently filtering 'intelligence' active participation in murder, coercion and dissolving antagonistic organisations. STOP

Brief: letter

Have dissolved eight agencies so far and five to go. Request permission to approach—Tuet Order KT, feld—SS Offizier Otto Rahn in South France ongoing excavation—Graal und treasure—schatz du Montsegur. STOP

Death report Constant Chevillion DOA krankenhaus—after 'Synarchic' trap triggered and successful. STOP

Having then waited a full seven minutes, one of the pilots got back into the aircraft and cranked up the Gems II turbines to a full 100 percent. He then executed a quick check of the systems prior to take off and waited.

The second pilot, meanwhile, shot one bullet into the rear tyre of the BMW, then quickly made his way back to the helicopter, which was now just ascending into the hover and was sitting approximately two feet off the hard standing. The pilot gave an out-of-character, impromptu salute then jumped on board.

Within thirty seconds, the Rolls Royce II, twin power train of the chopper had sparked up to over 109 % and the aircraft was almost out of sight. The two occupants of the car waited a few moments longer, then had taken a serious decision and risked turning over to observe what was going on around them.

The first occupant of the vehicle, who was dressed in an elegant and expensive Versace, grey suit, sat on the muddy road side with his head stuck deep in his arms for a moment, then began fumbling for his phone.

"What's wrong with you?" exclaimed his partner. The second man clearly appeared to be somewhat disturbed by the very quick and well-executed disruption he had just experienced.

"I am not sure but I think that could have been a simple summary execution of our lives. Helicopters don't fall out the sky like that, and the pilots of the British contingent of the Army Air Corps certainly do not point guns and pistols at civilians. Well, not without an amazingly high level of authority sanctioning such behavior, and they, now, the bastards, have got our map and SS documents.

I think we had better stand back from our pursuits. This is their way of warning us. This is their KT Order at work. Their inner network trying to scare us off! I think, at least for now, we should stay low, very low indeed. I don't fancy a rocket in my arse too soon. And, Colonel, we had better get another car; I think we have been very much compromised."

The man in the grey suit located his mobile phone and called his superior Officer for advice, then grabbed his Gestapo leather jacket and put it on.

Meanwhile, forty miles away the Lynx helicopter touched down on the warm tarmac on the east apron at RAF Leuchars' airfield, Fife, in Scotland.

CHAPTER TEN

Research—Ley lines

E rica Vine picked up her little red book and shuffled through the pages, she stopped and pondered on what Hastings had asked her to research. He had asked her to log events or coincidences that could be attributed to where an actual temple or church had been constructed, he asked for ledgers, older maps and land registers to be analysed and probable church locations over 300 years to be listed.

The world at large may be aware that 'Telluric ley lines' are lines not unlike the imaginary lines on a map—lines that run up and down and depict the northings and eastings, as on a normal road map for instance.

The information of which is then used in ascertaining one's position, when at sea or walking the land, of course most cars and boats these days are fitted with GPS—Global Positioning Systems or Google Earth databases, systems that automatically inform the user of where they are located digitally on the face of the planet. A luxury that was not afforded to the old world Knights' Templar Order.

Telluric ley lines are slightly different however from notional reference lines, as they are actual geophysical anomalies that appear to have a unique magnetic signature all of their own, a signature pulse that is known as the 'Rose Line' and the Templars had built many structures along these particular lines globally.

The questions that Erica was struggling with were: 'How did the ancient Order of nearly a thousand years ago know where these lines were? And how did they detect their presence?'

She flicked through a few more pages of the book then stopped again. She then searched the various words that alluded to church craft in general.

She had found the words 'Key Stone' several times in her search techniques and noted that it was a point where two ley lines physically albeit magnetically crossed or intersected; one such Key Stone is located right in the heart of Roslin Chapel in Scotland, which came as no surprise to the Historian.

She knew that the chapel itself had a significant relationship within the Order and one that was shrouded in either deliberate mis-direction or simply never existed in the first place. She instinctively knew that it would take more than a forty minute literal work-over to fully understand this very complex and highly explosive partnership between two super entities and she chose to follow the more direct route of learning.

Erica would admit that she herself never really understood what the full overarching relationship was with the Knights Templar Order and the Freemasons was per se, or what the Order was actually comprised of. Let alone the geophysical anomaly or the affiliation to the forces of Mother nature in general.

She moved on and reviewed other oddities such as things like Circadian Rhythms of where the detail explained that—'at an exact moment in time'—and untouched with repeatability and with accuracy, would define that organisms that live in a multi-climate could and would alter their own bio rhythms to suit the mode of the moment, or flip over their day and night relationships, or naturally alternate it's bodily chemicals mix over a 24 hour period to accommodate for reduced or increased melatonin levels.

The result can be dramatic and force an uncontrolled change in the animal as it adapts. A good example would be an animal's body temperature was automatically adjusted to suit both hot and cold conditions, or simply re-arrange it's eating and sleeping patterns.

Conversely, circadian rhythms in humans can be far more complex and affect change where the homosapien animal would—simply adjust accordingly and flip over to a nocturnal existence from a day time routine, and exist as such which can extend over a substantial period of time.

A further human example being the Inuit Eskimos, who live for extended periods of time in almost total darkness and survive quite well. Erica flicked over the cause and effect of the circadian rhythms in humans with the understanding that a range of biological markers were constantly at work informing the brain what actual time of the day it was. She scanned the complete document and suddenly paused at the word 'melatonin' again as it stuck out from the page of the leaflet for the umpteenth time. Then muttered away softly to herself.

"Wow, I never knew that melatonin is produced by the pineal gland, and that it has much lower levels during the daylight hours. Yet at night it increases its volume, however, if it was produced and introduced artificially into the body's blood stream then it induces natural sleep."

She wondered if the known enemies of the state would use this is a biological 'sleep' weapon and pondered on the notion that somehow these rhythms could be affected by the magnetic disturbance of the ley lines, especially as the low amount of metals in our bodies were magnetically sorted or pulled into place or forced into stimulation. Then the body would simply shut down and fall into slumber.

She read on and noted down a few more notes and recorded the date of the Chapel being founded in 1446 by Sir William Sinclair, she also discovered that the significance of the Rose can be seen within Western Gothic architecture, symbolizing the secrets of the divine feminine—and, the word Roslin as an example is the Polish name for flower and, 'Ross' is the Celtic or Scottish term for the colour red.

A colour denoting passion and blood and as ancient witches celebrated Beltane as being at one with Mother Nature. 'Tara' was a key time, and is known as such as one of the many cycles or festivals for the Wicca community or simply as the Witches' Corn Festival.

Which would witness masses of revelers coat themselves in red clay ochre and female bodily fluids, a process simply known as: Terr a-Ross. Then dance unceremoniously in the altogether having consumed a heady mix of herbs and perhaps alcohol in the process as a celebration to the cycles of human and animal life.

Erica shuddered a little at the thought of dowsing herself in any fluids let alone human Female ones, then jotted down four names of chapels that lay on the actual 'Ley Lines'

The locations consisted of Iona, Roslin, Columba and Kilmartin. She then closed her little red book and started to play around with a few of the letters which had been written down as a series scribbles next to a sketch of a single church, and was one of the documents that Hastings had passed on to her in order to aid and assist her in the research.

After a few minutes of table top scrabble and a moment of epiphany, to her surprise she quickly deduced that the term: 'LIONS ROCK IRL' was an anagram, or she had seen it written somewhere already. She flicked back over the pages and there it was sitting as a typed block text: + LIONS ROCK IRL+—as she thought next to a sketched drawing of the Roslin Chapel.

Erica had assumed that the term was something to do with a location somewhere in Ireland by the suffix IRL, but was completely wrong when she found out that the letters were actually the first three letters of each of the churches' names that she had just written down, and structures that were physically situated on these very complex 'Ley Lines' and again, of which, when the letters were unscrambled and pulled together alluded to the known: 'House of King Malcolm'—through which the Norwegian heraldry lineage was clearly defined.

"Goodness, just when you thought you knew something was on the ball, and almost one hundred per cent, suddenly it turns out to be the complete bloody opposite."

She huffed at her own ineptitude and inability to see the obvious and carried on with her research.

The understanding that the island of Iona had several Norwegian Kings and Queens interred on the hallowed grounds gave Erica good reason to shiver and a reason to dig a little deeper in her research. And she soon discovered that one of the Norwegian Kings had a son named 'Thorfinn'; born of the daughter of King Malcolm the II of Scotland, which appeared to have forged a long term Skandi, Ecosse relationship.

The street of the dead at the Abbey on Iona certainly could now boast full international acclaim.

Meanwhile, Hastings had made his way back to his flat after his fact finding country adventure and was sitting quietly on his soft sofa trying to work out his next course of action. He then picked up his laptop, sat cross legged on the floor, contemplating how Madelyn was reacting to current events as they unfolded. Especially since their last adventure as it was at the least a bit frantic and one of which had nearly got them both killed in the process.

She had already changed her eye colour with new contact lens inserts, giving her a sexier blue gaze; conversely, she had also dyed her long hair to almost pure blonde from the once fiery red mane.

He stared at her thinking how the woman he had met such a short time ago once exuded such a cool, confident and very sexy alluring manner, and yet, had now been forced to run and hide from an unprecedented evil, scurrying about the world like a scared rabbit and very vulnerable, and somehow Hastings took it on himself to ensure she came to no harm.

Let alone having to change her complete appearance to evade the outside world, Hastings gazed on, his mind began wandering toward her voluptuous curves that were now a major concern and conversation piece for the trappings of his fertile male mind.

She had been through so much lately and he just admired her for keeping her chin up and accepting what was going on around her. She momentarily stopped combing her hair then looked back at him then spoke.

"Hey, Kemp, do you think you could handle me as this slinky, sexy, blue eyed blonde, Meester Hastings?" she said, in a very sexy and seductive manner, whilst patting down her blouse top.

Hastings smirked at first followed by a huge grin. "Madelyn, I don't care what you look like, to me you are perfect. You have so much to offer the world, and I certainly can't complain about anything at the moment."

She then retorted, "So, do you think I can fool those Germans who keep following us?" Then began pushing her breasts together to try and make them look bigger or whatever it is that women want them to look like when men are around them.

He smiled again then took a deep breath. She smiled back at him then spoke again.

"Thank you for letting me stay over. I am also glad you are saying that, you are such a nice man. I don't often meet anyone who is so calm and generous as someone like you. The men I usually meet are caught up with their own worlds of depravity or deception and are generally full of shit, or are just simply morons."

Then she continued grooming herself.

"Thank you for that," he replied, as he wandered off to the bathroom. The Doctor continued combing her hair as Hastings returned to the room, found his laptop again, and searched the internet for an address.

"Voila! I think I have found what I was looking for!"

"What's that?" she responded, with a hint of general interest. Hastings pointed his finger in the air and spoke jubilantly.

"I, for once in my meager existence, may have just found the one source that could help us get out of this bind, and it has been an option at our disposal all of the time. I just never clicked on to it, because I am so close to the organisation, too close that I simply lost sight of it, or maybe too proud or too stupid to ask them for more help."

She stopped combing her hair. "Well who? Who is going to help us, Mr Stupido?"

Hastings pursed his lips and walked about the room straightening up some books up on the shelf, then sat a candle in the upright position in its ornate Egyptian holder.

"I have been so dumb, the KT's my Order! That's who can help us—my Grand Prior—he will have contacts who can arrange our short term dis-appearance, until we sort these people out."

Madelyn threw Hastings one of her most disgusting looks he had ever seen, and paused. "What!" she exclaimed. Then threw him a second, angered glare.

"I am not running away from this, now. We need to nail this problem once and for all. I have every intention of facing this German Teutonic or Black Cairo Lodge or whoever they are, face on, they need sorting out!"

Hastings was suddenly more abrupt in his response to Madelyn's comments and innocent ignorance as to how the secret Orders of the many Sects and Cults actually functioned, and he had to put her straight in her thinking and very quickly before she did something that could jeopardize them both.

"Darlene, you don't just deal with these institutions with a visit. These establishments make people go missing, and often in bizarre circumstances, remember Dr Toadie? Freddie? Even the established government offices of most countries dare not to pry when it concerns this type of event, or any mention of these so called establishments. People get edgy very quickly and often react the wrong way, and someone usually ends 'tits up' in a coffin. We need to call Gordy, and get some advice. He will know what to do?"

Unknown to Hastings, the Order had been planning to conduct a face to face with him regarding his current audit, and unplanned circumstances coupled with recent events had opened the doors of opportunity. The Grand Prior was just as amused by Hastings's phone call as was the investigator himself.

Madelyn glared her eyes again back at him, she knew he was right, but was so frustrated by the painfully slow process of information gathering. Then acting spontaneously without knowing the full outcome, and often too quickly to divert some other event from occurring.

"Shit, okay! So tell me what you have in mind . . . what do you suggest?" she asked.

Hastings flicked his mobile phone open then spoke softly into the Nokia handset.

"Hello, Cipher, its Kemp Hastings, Royal Lodge. I need some help!"

CHAPTER ELEVEN

Succession

O ne hour later, Hastings and the Doctor were sitting in the back seat of the black Mercedes Benz automobile speeding to a location that neither Hastings nor Dr Linn thought they knew even existed.

The driver of the Mercedes looked back at them a couple of times during the complete journey, and never spoke a single word throughout the trip, well that was until the driver told them to, rather abruptly, "Get out, of the car." Then directed them to walk to the set of steel gates a couple of hundred feet away.

Lying beyond the steel gates ran a single track way that led toward a very insignificant utility shed, a cubicle where the door appeared to be hanging on its supports more by desperation rather than being fixed to the door post by a robust set of screw-fix direct steel mounted bolts.

'If one walked through the gates and beyond the rickety shed, just a few hundred feet north then one would hit the edge of the large reservoir, and then get very wet,' thought Hastings, as he walked with a smirk running across his boyish face.

He stopped and gazed at the shed with a little more inquisitiveness.

"Not very impressive, but I wonder if it is not hiding one of those underground American nuclear command posts, you know like the ones that you see on the telly."

Approaching the door, he gently kicked the bottom of the wooden panel in order to dislodge it, or somehow make it swing into action. Instantly, he had to jump sideways as the bulk of the wooden door simply fell off its hinges completely, whereupon, in its downwards collapse, it nearly caught Madelyn in the process.

"That was clever, you big ape, that door nearly ripped my jacket," she cried out, hopping to one side, narrowly missing the protruding nails in the mason work by just a few inches. Hastings sprung to her aid. She turned and flashed him a very un-welcoming glare. He took the hint and backed off and began quizzing the shed again.

'Apart from what appears to be a new electrical fuse box and switch installation work, the shed is in a fair degree of disrepair and certainly is not used too often,' thought Hastings, as he stretched over the threshold and flicked the light switch to the 'on' position.

To their surprise the forty watt light bulb came on and the glass hissed a little as the damp was slowly turning into steam.

"Great for the night shift," he muttered, then leaned over to switch the lamp off

Madelyn, meanwhile, gave his jacket a slight tug and pointed to the left of the reservoir: standing several feet into the undergrowth, a soldier clad in British Army styled uniform stood quietly waiting and watching.

The soldier was clad in full camouflage gear and had emerged from the nearby hedge row almost undetected, and had watched as they assaulted the shed. Madelyn flinched uneasily as she spied the M1 carbine automatic machine gun that the soldier was holding.

"Mr Hastings!" The soldier was shouting just loud enough to catch his earshot. Hastings nodded his head in acknowledgment. Taking another quick glance around him the soldier beckoned the two to come forward and follow him.

The Doctor began counting her paces, and it was when she reached 189 steps that the soldier stopped, turned and then walked back towards them.

"Afternoon," he said, in a rather upper class aristocratic accent. "Damn shitty day to be walking in the woods don't you think, been waiting for you chaps quite a bit of time now, but you're here now, that's all that matters. Did you get lost or something on the way?"

No answer came, and the soldier pointed up the pathway with the barrel of his machine pistol.

"It's just beyond the tree line over there, toward the big house," remarked the soldier. Then he walked off back into the greenery of the forest.

"Mmmmh!" Hastings muttered.

"I thought that was no ordinary run-of-the-mill squaddie. This is all very strange. I would have placed him definitely as a Captain or a Major, especially the way he wore his beret, too scruffy to be a Tom. You know, Maddy, I think things are actually getting better, what I mean by that, is that to be met by a full military chap who could actually be a Major or even a Colonel, is all a bit more serious."

Madelyn turned and smiled. "Pompous ass," she thought, then gave a quick thought to their predicament.

Having made their way to the entrance vestibule of the manor house, Hastings had the most peculiar bout of déjà vu. He explained to Madelyn that he had walked in these grounds before or he thought he might have done, but that was at least 15 years ago, and recalled he was here as a guest at an impromptu dinner party having solved what was a fabricated hoax for some weird oriental weapons scam or other, but he recalled he was very well paid, and got very drunk.

"Mr Hastings, Lieutenant Colonel James Graham-Marquis, Army Air Corps special Ops, been watching you for a while, and the good Doctor, Miss Linn glad you are still alive. How do you do?" he said, presenting a hand for shaking. "I have been given rather an odd set of orders from Whitehall this morning, it appears the establishment has unwanted guests in their midst, and they don't want any interference until the Order has settled some rather slightly embarrassing business, and certainly do not want any negativity until those damn internal elections are finished.

We first caught sight of those 'left wing fanatics' when you went to visit that dead preacher chap, the cleric—whatshisname . . . damn—what was his name? Ah, yes! Niven. Dear old boy. Keeled over with a heart attack, oddly, just after you left him. Bloody unfortunate timing though. I hope he gave you what you needed Mr Hastings, as we are burying the old boy tomorrow, well at least the Order are interring him at half two tomorrow, St John's chapel Marykirk or Laurencekirk, not quite sure which one is which. Anyway, all shitty stuff I am afraid. I mean if those fanatics had got to him first, then we could have been having a very different conversation."

Hastings shook his head.

"I take it they are not of the Teutonic Order from Koln then?"

The Officer removed his hat, then spoke softly. "They are no more members of an Order of the Temple than Sweeney Todd or Jack the Ripper were, Mr Hastings, they have probably had a distant affiliation somewhere along the line and somehow got their hands on an old World War II map and a Nazi message thingy and sparked their madcap idea of treasure seeking. Anyway, they are just lunatic gold diggers and they are bloody damn dangerous too. Our man in the sky says he was tempted to shoot them both when he had the chance—just the other day when you were out at the 'Devil's Bridge Chapel'." The Officer cut himself short in his upper class, verbal ramblings and changed the subject as one of the stewards approached them.

"Should be a good bash though the Grand Master is doing the honours. It will be a low key affair, just the select few from the Grand council and some of the key players from the local Order attending, and you must be there, Mr Hastings, the request hails from on high. So until then, you may stop over here in our little hideaway, we have a modest safe house here for you both, can't have the Germans running riot and chasing you around the countryside every twenty minutes, no! That just will not do.

Now, Miss Linn, if I can direct you towards those four ladies in the foyer over there if you will. These ladies will take care of all your needs, and please do not worry—they are real nurses. They are from the Woman's Royal Army Corps or Women's institute, one of the two, but, they are serving soldiers and I believe there is also a ladies' powder room and gymnasium somewhere on the second level."

Madelyn smiled politely back at the Officer, thinking that he was perhaps having a go at her voluptuous size 12 body and her flabby thighs with his fleeting comment towards the gymnasium. But she still harboured the thought that he was indeed still a complete pompous ass."

She thought again, smiled then walked into the anti-chamber with the girls.

The Officer, meanwhile, placed a hand on Hasting's shoulder and motioned him into the opposite reception room.

"So down to business, Mr Hastings, may I call you Kemp? You must meet with the Grand Master as soon as possible he has some information and knowledge to impart to you. I think the helicopter crew are picking him up sometime this evening about eightish, do you fancy a pint?"

The Colonel then pressed the buzzer on the wall. A few moments later, another steward dressed in military mess dress appeared from a nearby doorway and took their order for drinks.

CHAPTER TWELVE

Service of Departure

The service was a very dignified occasion and the good, proud standing Pastor was committed to God in Templar time honoured tradition, the simple, oak coffin had been draped with the Templar banner and cross-patterned flag, and was sitting on a set of silver tressels. The six Pall bearers standing quietly with bowed heads waiting for the service to begin.

The Grand Master gave an exemplary well-rehearsed speech and provided an overview of the late vicar's loyalty to the Order ending in a bout of prayer and admiration for a fallen brother.

After a series of salutes and readings by a few of the assembled Grand Knights, the old vicar was finally laid to rest. His mortal life having been recited by the people who knew him best—The Knights' Templar.

The Arch Bishop and the Grand Chaplain both stood in front of the grave and each spoke in turn as Grand Master gathered the Templar flag together.

The Chaplain stepped forward and blessed the coffin and recited a few simple chosen words: "Knights and Dames, our departing brother has cast off his 'arming jacket' and has donned the veil of death as he walks from this world to the next.

Our home spun Castellan has donned the mantle and surcoat of the Lord above and now serves him as a new soul and soldier of Christ. I will now read a short passage extracted from the Templar book of rule;—rule 277.

Let us pray: Receiver, we beseech you, O' Lord this your servant fleeing to you from the tempests of this world and the snares of the devil, so that having been received by you he may enjoy both protection in the present world and reward in the world to come through Christ, Amen."

"Chevaliers, graveside salute swords at the ready," came the call from the Grand Prior himself acting Master of Ceremonies. In the near distance, a lone Scottish piper piped the last post and a few bars from the 'Lost Gospel of St John'.

A haunting melody echoed across the glen as an eerie squeal of a lone hawk echoed across the cemetery as the coffin touched down on terra firma, and Vicar Niven was finally laid to rest in the auld kirk yard, just as the minister had requested.

He was now resting on God's hallowed ground after his 89 years on the planet. He rests with his dear departed spouse and Dame—Lady Jane Fotheringay."

The service ended.

Hastings was naturally placid through the whole ceremony which was conducted in relative silence, lock stock and barrel. And it had caught him on the hop as the actual ceremony itself was not his forte, and he found no solace or peace in such uncanny circumstances of ceremony, sometimes, he would say it was all a bit too macabre and bizarre for his liking.

But he fully accepted this parting ritual as crucial in bringing the higher echelons of the Order together to pay their respects and he wondered why he had somehow been caught up within this complex Templar tapestry.

The Grand Master himself was a tall chap and towered over Hastings by a good four inches, Hastings's first impression was that the man was very clean and suave with a heavy crop of wavy light brown hair and appeared to be very wise and educated.

After a few moments, Hastings then added a few other ramblings of his thinking toward the Grand Master's psychological make-up in general, and what he thought was open for discussion. Perhaps, he, the Grand Master possessed a slight hint of megalomaniac tendencies with a pinch of narcissistic behaviour, as pre-requisites for the role. If Hastings was to be brutally honest, he struggled to pigeon hole this very interesting man precisely.

Apart from the fact that he spoke with a soft tone of voice that exuded total clarity and directness he was quite in control of his surroundings and the people he interfaced with, this was an example of a strong man who knew what he wanted, and a leader who knew how to obtain it, and no one was going to stand in his way.

The Grand Master stood and watched as Hastings approached him, then extended his hand to say hello.

"Brother Hastings, great to meet you at last. Sadly, not the most ideal venue, nor the occasion, I had wished for. I have heard so much about you, and thank you for staying for the ceremony. You have had a rather interesting year, don't you think?

I simply cannot believe or comprehend how you have managed to solve all those mysteries so quickly, oh! And before I forget, that reminds me I have something for you. This trinket was given to me two weeks ago by a very senior member of the RC church; sorry for the delay, but this is quite an honor for me to actually pass this on to you, the Vatican wants you to have this.

The Grand Master passed a small red box to Hastings at the graveside, then shook his hand again, it was then that the assembled funeral party had started making their way back into the chapel house annex, and waited patiently for the after ceremony to begin with the customary red wine and chit chat—of course the inner conclave took time to consume bread and water as a pre cursor part of ritual then joined the main reception.

"Thank you," he replied, slipping the small ring box into his jacket pocket. The Grand Master stopped, turned and faced Hastings straight on.

"It's not every day one receives a duplicate ring of a past Pope, Mr Hastings, even we as Grand Masters do not receive such worldly rewards. Our records show that only one other person had received a token of thanks directly from Rome itself, and that Knight was Andre' Montbard, of course before he became Grand Master, you join an elite select few Brother Kemp, well done, well done indeed. The Holy See are indeed a strange bunch of vicars and clerics, but I think they mean well, even if they can be so damn bloody single minded on some of their homespun views. Anyway, let us discuss your succession for a moment or two shall we . . . are you ready to take the mantle of succession Brother Hastings?"

Hastings was caught on the hop. He was not really sure what this meant, considering his understanding of being placed seemingly at a lower down level in the order of rank and file as a mere 'sword bearer' and as an investigator in the actual Templar Order, which itself was not a structured role. And he pondered for a moment or two on the pecking order of succession.

It was then that the two were joined by three other Knights who had entered the vestry of the small church, each man clad in full Knights Templar regalia. Hastings was momentarily fixed; somehow he knew a day like this would occur, but not so bloody soon.

The Grand Master spoke with an even softer tone as he explained some of his current concerns. "The Order has lost three executive officers in as many days and we have had to move quickly".

The Grand Master reflected on a few points about the investigator and the auditor traditional setup approach to recruitment, where a much quicker level of exposure to the internal workings of the Order are placed as it were on a silver platter for the chosen recipient—and many doors just seemingly threw themselves open for both travel and career succession.

Hastings was of the right age and maturity and he possessed a wealth of experience having investigated and documented his many adventures in his scribblings, especially as an avid amateur author of folklore and myths. But, more importantly, as he documented the Knights' Templar history, and, of course its established workings.

And he had now to simply accept that his many global travels were not just coincidence, but an orchestrated effort to gain as much exposure to the hidden Order as permissible.

He had become an eminent scholar of Templar life and had proven many times over that he was capable of looking after the Order's interests. The Grand Master placed a hand on his shoulder and spoke. "As you have already met the military arm of our Order, I won't dwell too much on the finer detail of office suffice to say, please don't be deceived, they are not full British Army, they are the only private army in Europe that serve our needs, and they belong to the Earl Mar and the Earl of Atholl.

These families have held a Scottish military office within our ranks for a very long time now, and we could go back to Balantrodoch seventeen hundred and something, in our records. Half of Atholl's soldiery is ex-serving SAS men or specialist marines, damn decent lot and they stick to what they know best, soldiery and protection. Mar's lot, on the other hand, they are more technical types. Did you know that he has four helicopters and a few motor boats and other craft at his disposal? That kind of thing at his fingertips, costs a bloody fortune to buy let alone maintain.

I think they are those Lynx type attack machines, seen them on the telly, all impressive stuff. But all that aside, we, on the other hand, need outstanding officers of the inner conclave, officers to manage our business and orchestrate such things as marine and aviation activities and of course protecting relics my Brother, and we think, Mr Hastings, you step up to that particular mark, and, of course we know your particular niche is logic."

Hastings thought for a few moments then asked a question. "Tell me, Grand Master, surely you have other Order members who fit the bill?"

The Grand Master sniffed a wee sniff of fresh air then pinched his nose whilst glancing upwards. "If I was lucky enough to have several men of your character Mr Hastings then that would not be an issue, and we would not be having this conversation. But, we simply don't have the modern day resource. Grandfather's rites or succession rights are what are keeping us afloat at the moment, just as your grandfather had done and had placed you within our order. You should read the 'rule' of our domain now and again, because in your case Templar rule number: 337 applies. Don't worry you won't have to remember them all, there are only two hundred and forty-three that apply to our modern order, but it is always good to know what you are actually supposed to know. So, please do myself and the Order the honour of accepting our invitation and join the inner master's conclave?"

Just then the two Knights in the form of the Grand Seneschal and the Grand Prior of Scotland began walking towards them. The Grand Prior invited them forward. Then they all entered the confines of the inner annex where the modestly furnished room had been lavishly laid out for post ceremonial 'afters' and of which several bottles of Champagne had been neatly laid out along six long wooden tables. They both nodded toward the GM and moved on.

The Stewards were busy sitting some of the Vicar's family down and catering for requests for water or napkins. Hastings was to sit at the end of the table and momentarily thought about being a new military mess member and Mister Vice and had to toast his rise in the ranks. Somehow this was very different.

The Grand Master turned to Hastings and the other Knights and although he was still talking very softly, his voice was clear and concise. The assembled group listened without interruption. "Gentlemen, accompany me if you will."

The three then walked towards the assembled members of the inner conclave. Hastings appeared to be very confused, everyone around him seemed to somehow understand what was going on, but he remained in a state of limbo trying to fathom why he was being introduced to his peer group by the Grand Master himself.

"You know these Dames and Brethren of course?" He posed with an odd sort of louder tone. "These brave men and ladies will support your every move and decision, even this wonderful man and Grand Prior has his limitations, but he will serve the Order well and remain loyal into his aged years, as I think most of us will. May I present the higher Order team?"

The Grand Master gradually walked past each member and bid them all a very warm face-to-face welcome. He then introduced specific members of conclave to Kemp Hastings:

Brother Hastings this is the Grand Marshal—Chev (Lt Col) Grahame, Marquis, you have of course met the Colonel recently and he will perhaps become more strategic as you conduct your important task of our review. Hastings nodded having met the Officer recently.

We also have our Grand Seneschal—Chevalier Robert, Scott-Walters, Bob is our intellectual guru he has a knowledge base we depend upon, what Bob does not know about the Vatican you can place on a s stamp.'

Hastings nodded and presented his hand for Shaking,'

'Nice to meet you' He said then acknowledged that the handshake was strange, had Bob lost two fingers or was he telling him something different. Hastings just smiled and followed the Grand Master into the halls. The trio then moved toward the top table and waited as the assembled parties took their seats. The GM continued in his recital to Hastings.

"There are some real Scottish history amongst these ranks, Brother Hastings, the names alone are very synonymous with our Order's turbulent history, but we have a lineage that is unrivalled in any establishment worldwide. Of course, each one of our Knights and Dames are custodians of our wealth. Admittedly some hold more than others. The Grand Seneschal, as an example, he holds the jewelry of Sheba, although the Order did indeed return a few of her other significant pieces back to Axum. On the other hand, our very own Grand Prior here, well, he has more fun in his role. He has a lot to generally contend with, not only as the controller of ancient documents that cement the Order together, but the headache of all that damn war gold he has to move around periodically and a couple of castles to organise, I think. Great wealth Brother Hastings and the warring factions out there 'in hostile land' are still trying to acquire it.

Hastings was suddenly taken by surprise as he caught sight of Erica and Madelyn standing side by side within the ranks of the assembled group. He had no inclination that these two Dames had recently migrated into the Order and had taken posts as Grand Order representatives. He was excited and full of admiration for them both. But could not understand why Erica had said nothing about her admission into the ranks.

The Grand Master continued with his little speech and physically touched Hastings several times on the arm and his head as he discussed the proud moments that the Order had celebrated. Not only in glorious battle moments but in their global achievements, but the Order's charitable footprint that served the world at large.

The GM took time for reflection sipped his champagne then spoke again. "That is why we are the Knights Templar, Ecosse, and one of our great members and Grand masters was chosen as no other than Charles Edward Stuart himself. He held office from the 24th day of September 1745, and I can tell you something, I wish I had been at that particular meeting. I will tell you this, it must have been utter chaos and sheer pandemonium when he took office.

What an event to have been a fly on the wall; Holyrood palace in Edinburgh was buzzing like a fairground in full swing as the new laws of the land of this new doctrine of Unionism was being argued and discussed in heated debate. Unlike the dried out, dribble drabble, boyish, boring politics we witness today.

But back then it was hard arsed politics and face-to-face aggressive dialogue tackling the complicated subjects of politics head on. Discussions that changed the course of Scottish and European history itself, a fight against the infidel and other enemies of the State, discussions fuelled by passion and hatred along with spiteful revenge, albeit, often at sword point. Many thought the Union would never evolve, but it did. Charles Edward Stuart, Grand Master, was installed into the Order on that very same night as the 'Sovereign Grand Master'. No-one dared oppose this unprecedented decision for his appointment, especially as a great battle had just been won at Prestonpans and the Scottish Royals were jubilant."

The newly installed Sovereign Grand Master was not alone. He had some very clever and brave men around him, for one, the infamous, The Duke of Montrose a 'proddie' who kept his Templar oath, quite strange for a protestant to do this but he did, and survived quite well until he directly opposed the infamous John Knox at his own peril and perished as a result.

"So you see, my Brother, you join a very long line of succession and an elite few who have been chosen to serve our Order. We have a rather special role for you to play within our Order Brother, however, I am sure your Grand Prior will lay out all the details over the next couple of days. So, how does that sound Brother Hastings? We might even draw you a handsome salary to help things along a little," remarked the Grand Master, nodding toward the Grand Prior who waited with baited breath for Hastings to accept his invitation.

Hastings knew or at least thought he knew where he stood as far as the Order was concerned, and he now realised that he had given himself little credit or no real self-appraisal or pats on the back for his work over the past few years on their behalf.

He had taken time to absorb the Order's business and slowly worked things out. He had learned how it actually functioned. He could rest on his laurels for a short time, especially through his unique authorship in documenting The Knights' Templar inner workings.

But similarly, he was very humbled to have been even asked to join the upper echelons of control and as yet, still had no idea of what role he was actually to perform was.

He also knew this would be a great move in as much to show the external world at large that he possessed a considerable amount of internal knowledge as to how the Order functioned. But more importantly understood the politics involved in dealing with such a multinational entity.

Albeit, he had no idea what the relationship with the Mar's and Atholl's Armies had to do with the good old British Army, let alone the Order per se, and now, this was all new information he had to absorb and log into his library of understanding.

He would have to conduct some further research into funding and daily expenses that an Army cost to maintain, let alone comprehend the amount of wealth that was at stake, especially now as the order moved its assets between global locations.

Hastings, by all definitions, was one of a handful of people who possessed the intellectual property that the Order had almost failed to keep alive within their ranks. He assumed that having a private Army at your fingertips and disposal could help with security issues and their hierarchy stemmed to international commanders.

The Grand Master watched and listened as Hastings recited what he knew about how the early Order came together in the year 1127, and after a series of attacks on pilgrims who ventured as far as the holy land, who were constantly attacked until a group of French mercenaries decided to protect the pilgrims whilst working under the watchful eye of one Hugues De Payen.

Hugues De Payen was the one man who took steps to build an empire under the tenure of a succession of Popes who backed the Knights in their holy duties to protect Christendom, and it was due to his extreme skills in man management to convince his peer group to join him, and his business acumen to make it worthwhile.

The Grand Master listened with interest for a short period of time then spoke. "Brother Hastings, one has to understand that we as an Order have not always been as squeaky clean as history may depict. We have to remain mindful that we were mercenaries, we were the armed forces of the day, simple killing machines back then, and we as an Order during the tenure of Pedro de Montagu (1219-1230)—as an example were captured in the middle of an outright holy crusade, which in essence meant a great deal of warfare, and obviously death destruction, bloodshed and despair. It was during the year 1221, that we as an Order became very greedy internally and had to impose several new strict rules to stem our own officers' activities, squires and members and curb their selfish activities.

These new rules were enforced like no others rules such as: addendum—number 78 as an example, 'about sharing our pack horses with all the order,' or rule: 90 in order to help and assist castle households or Castellans—a place where Templar belongings were moved to for security purposes, and were moved around the countryside in order to equally balance off the inventory, albeit in a fair and just custodial process. It all takes careful planning you know, and if personnel get greedy then we have to deal with them swiftly whilst exercising fairness also. There were perhaps too many Knights ostracized for all the wrong reasons during this time, and perhaps even today globally we may have some issues to deal with.

Some of our rules are extant today, some are quite potent. Rule 244 for example where it states: 'If greed within the order was rife and brothers who did not share their inventory with other brothers, then they (the offenders) would be stripped of their habit and any rites.' But conversely, rules 200 through to 309 are clear about our brotherly conduct toward each other and our squires.

I am, however, glad to say that we have matured over the past seven hundred years. But please believe me when I say, the killing still continues in the name of Christendom in this very volatile modern world, and that alien Armies are still at logger heads with themselves to gain control, and when you look at contemporary events balanced against history face on.

Well! Nothing has really changed globally since 1127, has it? Goodness, we are still fighting in Afghanistan and Syria, and of course some of the other Arab League of Nations are still in turmoil and dis-array with no support from neighbouring countries, less for Jordan, but that is of course because of the footprint of Christendom.

Greed for wealth and power Brother Hastings, that's all it is, the sanctity of human life has left their immediate concern and have eroded away, and, are now distant thoughts, and, they the 'infidel' have not learned a single lesson about people since the early crusading years.

We, however, as an Order must maintain stability in the more democratic countries of the world, and this is where we concentrate our efforts wholesale. Tell me? Have you ever been to St Petersburg or Porto in Portugal yet Brother?" asked the Grand Master, rubbing a single gold coin around in the palm of his hand.

"And, I believe you want some more information on these elusive German coins and gold bullion. Well, they are of course as you can imagine a bit of an accountancy conundrum for us all. You see we cannot simply melt them down as they are war trinkets, and we certainly can't sell them on eBay as seconds now can we?"

The Grand Master smiled, exposing a very healthy well-kept set of dentures, and almost gave out an unhealthy spurt of laughter. "We have too much to deal with my friend, but five years from now things should be very different, we can apply to the war commission to exonerate our holdings and release some of the deposits for melt down or public disposal, I mean for the Order it all goes back into charity. That means, Brother Hastings, we have a couple of tons of gold to play with, and we will require good Officer's to manage its dissemination. This will be very exciting times don't you think?"

After a couple hours of reflection and a healthy sit down meal, the Grand Master then said his thank yous and good byes in one presentation, and asked that all members of the assembled Knights and Dames enjoy the banquet in the memory of the late Pastor and Grand Chaplain Dr Niven-Airlie.

As the helicopter approached from nowhere, the Grand Master stood up raised a hand and gave a parting statement, "Remember, ladies and gentlemen, our rules are there to be obeyed, not to be broken in any shape or form, that's the job of our Politicians. Please remember that our 'Knights' Templar Rules' have been in force since the council of Troyes declared them legal, and that was a very, very long time ago. So, please, raise your goblets and glasses in memory of the Grand Chaplain, and glory to the Holy Order."

After the salutation, the Grand Prior requested that all Knights be up-standing and then saluted the Grand Master as he left the building under the heavy escort of the homespun Scottish contingent of the Temple's secret Army.

CHAPTER THIRTEEN

Vaults and Coffers

D octor Erica Vine of the GUE waited patiently by the gates to the old St Mary's Steeple, Dundee, the Church itself being a medieval structure, circa 13th century that stood high proud in the busy High Street of the city of discovery.

The structure perhaps boasting more history than the older town's complete history all put together, especially since being sacked by both William Wallace and King Edward II—The Longshanks, during the bloody tenure of the English King.

Erica Vine was a plain Jane kind of woman who possessed a wicked sense of detail, her analytical eye missed nothing, and she was a fantastic source of information regarding metallurgy and science fact that Hastings was simply blown away by.

Hastings admired her for many things and perhaps her slim elegant figure coupled with her mousy brown hair helped a wee bit, not to mention her well-developed bosom.

Her presence and voluptuous figure he had recognised instantly during the Grand Master's line up at the funeral gathering. Erica had somehow joined the ranks of the order which was a good thing, as Hastings had been momentarily reminded of the resources that surrounded him.

Hastings had arranged a meeting with Erica to discuss some jewelry that was reported to belong to the Queen of Sheba and he wanted it authenticated on the 'QT', as it were, as part of the internal review and his Templar audit scope.

His earlier meeting with the cleric and information source was a very strange one indeed, and now that he was dead it was almost impossible to address any of the issues they had discussed.

Hastings was thinking about his comments, and had aimed his thoughts at the windows of the churchyards, not only for Roslin but another church's stained glass windows across at Angus, located deep in the mearns. And he knew he had to visit Cults, Maryculter in Aberdeen, and Balantrodoch, a village nearer the borders of Scotland and England at some point.

The source for the artifact was a well-known local and very dead clergy man: Norman Niven-Airlie, who apparently hailed from somewhere nearer to the glens of Clova in and around Castle Airlie, some forty miles away from his own apartment at the manse in Farnell, and why Hastings was coerced to travel to the middle of Fife to meet the old man nearer to the Kilmartin and Roslin chapel's was a matter for further discussion and was not a normal decision for him to make.

But somehow on that occasion it seemed the right thing to do, as he was engaged by the Order itself, and it was also another opportunity to visit the home of the St Clair family.

The clergyman had expressed his sincere intentions to protect and to preserve the artifacts from the onset of their meeting, and as part of the assignment he had been tasked to protect these holy items with his life if need be, and now he had done so for the last forty years.

His home at Kilmartin church was his retreat, and his other home in Angus was his day job, or that's what the cleric would say if he was still alive.

But he knew back then that he was getting old and was quite frail. This was worrying for the old cleric and he was thinking about insurances where his physical health had become a concern in order to keep to his vow to the Order; a concern of integrity as part of the internal mechanics of the Order. The old man also knew that Hastings was being groomed for bigger and better things, albeit Hastings himself had no idea that he was being systematically indoctrinated to perform a specific function for the Holy Order.

The old man had furnished Hastings with a simple list and requested that he take time to meet the other keepers and ask the questions that needed to be asked regarding the audit that he was undertaking.

He recalled that the list was a simple A4 normal sheet of paper with a few names scribbled upon it, and stark reflection of modern times pitched against those ancient of days, when things like pieces of paper and communications had evolved to almost 'persona non gratis, level and very informal, almost inducing anonymity. After their healthy discussion they drove a few short miles to a more significant chapel at old Roslin.

The old man had finished up the remainder of his talk as they walked through the chapel grounds, and then thanked Hastings for his time. The old cleric then pointed the auditor in the direction of the 'auld' chapel. Hastings recalled the look on the old man's tired face; it was one of sincerity and the utmost honesty.

The main door to the chapel had been left ajar. Hastings walked forward and gingerly pushed through the doorway pushing the heavy wooden door inwards then stepped into the main entrance hallway, and momentarily caught sight of the overhead sign in his peripheral vision it read: 'Visitor Reception Area'.

After what seemed an eternity, still no one came. So he decided to move on and make his way across the building into the central aisle of the old chapel. He then stood absolutely motionless and awestruck absorbing the magnificent architecture, symbology, effigies and inscriptions again.

Many notions of intrigue, mystery and hidden secrets were running rife through his hippocampus; each idea favouring his intellectual investigative threads, which were now sprinting off in all kinds of directions, and he was simply overwhelmed by the enormity of the internal architecture of the building.

It was all too much for him to take in for one sitting; he had visited this chapel many times before, and yet it still had the same effect on him, he found a chair nearby then sat down staring up at the central keystone rose for several minutes.

"These German morons cannot be even allowed to think about removing that little beauty, let alone permit these damn visitors to consider destroying the chapel for their greedy purposes.

The whole place would probably collapse inwards," he muttered under his breath then threw his attentions at the distant stained glass window. Once he had settled his emotions, Hasting wandered almost aimlessly through the house of God pondering for a moment on the few hero Knights who were interred below the church, and contemplated for a few moments what real secrets they may be hiding. He remained mindful that behind the Templar traditions caves and vaults were the best locations to protect and preserve relics.

The Templar Cross—
Ref: OSMTH Archive 2012

Hastings stood at the base of the 'Apprentice Pillar', slap bang opposite the ornate altar, and took a very long deep breath as he stared at the awesome and intricate carvings that made up this very 'one off' sculpture of what he could only describe as a helix, that encapsulated the upright solidity of the standing masonry.

He then began muttering away to himself, "Hiram Abif, would have simply been bowled over by this place, even he as the grandest of architects would bow to such a majestic piece of ornate stonework, a monument only fit for a prince or indeed a king."

Being informed as Hastings was, he took even more time to deliberate his attentions toward the octagonal base of the pillar and recalled his referencing towards the eight-pointed cross that the Order had adopted as it official logo.

Somewhere along the historical time line—the cross was made up from the conventional cross design around about the year 1324, and signified continuity up into the 21st century. The real question that hangs on the lips of many historians and archaeologists was: 'What lies beneath the octagonal base of the apprentice pillar?'

Perhaps the head of a biblical figure the secrets of Christendom or something more exclusive. Hastings opinion was that the actual mathematics of the structure was based around the shape of the octagon and the cross was derived as the ultimate compass within its concentric footprint, providing what could be seen as an equal balance of distance and scale.

He knew his thoughts and suggestions were not new ideas but his own interpretation of his understanding of symbology often led him up a very long dark and often fruitless path, and he would be the first to admit that when he got it wrong, which was at least 80 percent of the time, he got it grossly and monumentally wrong.

But, conversely when he got things correct, well, that was indeed a different matter entirely, and has led him to many hidden obscure riches over the years. He traversed the inside of the ornate chapel with a boyish smirk spread across his inquisitive face and perhaps on this occasion knew the chapel better than most of his peers.

Suddenly, for some insane reason, he thought about his last visit to the distant structure at Brechin and the first cathedral with a beautiful Minaret tower, in Angus. A building which boasted humble medieval origins whilst still remaining the oldest structure in the known burgh, and of course, constructed on an older Celtic monastery site.

It was under the archaic tenure of King Kenneth II of Scotland circa 971-995 giving this great city in a monastic guise to the Lord, endowing the community of Christendom with lands and notoriety, and thus, had the church built to satisfy demand.

The local monks of the day were known as 'Culdee' and help preserved the copious amount of ancient carvings and medieval sculptures that lay within God's house. An important artefact known as the 'St Mary's' stone was dug up in a local garden in the earlier part of the eighteenth century and one of the earliest examples of Latin inscription, coupled with an effigy of St Mary and the infant Christ surrounded by other evangelistic figures.

Brechin Cathedral boasts a high 'round tower' not dissimilar to a modern day mosque tower and many odd grave stones in the shadows of the Cathedral have been discovered in the passage of time, however a distinct hogsback was discovered—a style of grave epitaph dated from about the 11th century and denoted Norwegian or Swedish origin, as the script was clearly written in Norse Ringerike, along with other examples of grave stones, some of which depict a Romanesque font which clearly defines that this Cathedral's influence had reached perhaps as far abroad as the Holy Land itself.

Hastings recounted the history of the Cathedral whilst recalling the origins of the Church itself and had seen a parchment signed by King David I, during his tenure and the King asked the Diocese of Brechin and its representative Bishop Samson to make changes to the structure.

History tells us that in the year 1225 the Culdees' Monks were replaced by Canons and a smaller Cathedral was built in Gothic style. The building we observe today was completed several centuries later, circa 1300, through to 1398.

Later in time, as the building evolved, a considerable amount of damage was made as subsequent changes and alterations were conducted bringing the building to its current un-natural state. Not unlike most churches of our day.

As a building that was testament to the treatment of time, the structure has survived relatively well, and was once dedicated to the Holy Trinity and blessed with a coat of arms.

Hasting's coughed a few spurts then wiped his nose just as he thought about the 'Coat of Arms' itself.

"Damn, very different from Brechin. How the hell did I miss that?"

Hastings walked through the upper levels of the museum, then extended his visit to Roslin Chapel to include the local graveyards

"Shit what did that poem say? Three down, three deep and three across, then thy door shall prevail. Oh, yeah there it is." Then he wandered off toward the castle walls.

CHAPTER FOURTEEN

Reichsbank Coinage

A s Hastings approached the old Steeple, he noticed Erica instantly. She had not really changed that much since their last investigation encounter, and after a fleeting hello at the Dr Niven's funeral, Hastings recalled their last adventure together and an errand which brought them together as a team to investigate the discovery of two 12th century swords and several artifacts from the same period.

They had embarked on a spontaneous visit to one of Scotland's famous land mark Castle's located at Loch Leven in Fife, an excursion as part of their investigation on behalf of the Fisher Kings which nearly got them both murdered as a result.

He gave her the customary once over, she looked good—she looked quite desirable. As his mind wandered, he then drifted to the land of where getting slapped in the face was the most common outcome if women could read a man's most inner thoughts. He smiled as she appeared out of the doorway of the NEXT shop in the shopping store.

'Looks like she has matured a little too,' he thought to himself and muttered away to no-one in particular as she approached.

She also appeared to have more meat on the proverbial bone, as it were. From what he could recall, she had filled out nicely since their last encounter, and she had obviously been working out, as her well-developed 'buxom' bosom appeared to be more to Hasting's physical and sexual preference.

He always thought that women should be built like a woman: not scraggy, skinny, or have an overdeveloped passion to visit McDonalds but with a shapely and full figure. An example would be a middle aged woman who worked out and looked after herself.

He then smiled one of his welcoming big, broad grins alluding to, 'How have you been, babe?' kind of smiles and bid her good day

"Hey, Erica, you're looking very stylish, dear lady. And looking rather hip too. So, how have you really been? How's your sex life?" he said, trying to provide her with a barrage of questions to relieve any potential tension that may have still existed. Erica gave him a welcome glance and turned a slight embarrassing red colour, then kissed him on both cheeks.

"Kemp Hastings, you are still full of it shit aren't you? Always so nice and polite and very direct. Actually, I am fine, and anyway more to the point how is your sex life?"

There was a nice warm, almost tangible pause as both parties exchanged smiles and pleasantries. Then Erica spoke. "I have been working away at some project stuff, basically getting on with my life. I have been researching some Japanese jewelry from the Genpei war period, really interesting stuff. And I can see you have added a few pounds to your middle aged spread too," she said, sticking a finger into the middle of his stomach just under his waistcoat.

"Yep, you got me there. I have delved into the deepest depths of McDonald's. Did you know they do breakfast as well? Bloody marketing genius. Anyway still consuming copious amounts of brandy and Carlsberg these days, you know me I will never change. But first I have sent you a little trinket in the post. It's the Sheba tiara. If you could give it the once over I would be very appreciative."

She smiled again. "Yep, that's no problem. The Ethiopian team are very quick to authenticate relics. We have a crown and necklace already. Should get it done by the end of the week." She pursed her lips and smiled again, thinking he may be 'pigging out' but he had somehow still managed to maintain a male and desirable physique, and still well-acceptable in her eyes.

"Well that's good news, mustn't let yourself go, Kemp. You will just end up old and wrinkly—just like all those chips you have eaten. And, I hear you have a new partner as well. Does she like chips? I hope she is keeping you on the straight and narrow and out of trouble?"

Hastings said nothing and placed an arm around her slim waist as they walked toward the car park. "Yes and no, Erica. An amazing young girl called Madelyn Linn. She is a biblical studies teacher, and an amazing source of information. Just like you. You will meet her later today, hopefully. She is researching some church archives for me. Anyway, more about you. Are you back at St Andrews yet? Or have you ostracized yourself completely from them these days?" he asked, poking fun at her new found career, and pointed to the wooden bench in the parkway. "Can we sit in the open on the bench I like to watch the pigeons fight for chips and things, and I fear I am always being watched these days; I must be getting paranoid or something," he said, motioning her again to take a seat near the museum entrance.

Then Erica explained a few other events in her interrogative biblical life. "Actually, I am doing some part time tutorials for their new science and art fair as well. I am told that it will all will kick off in a few months' time. Seems odd really, but they want to mix contemporary art and ancient history for the new Victoria and Albert museum exhibition—that new complex that they are building on the wharf here in Dundee."

Hastings nodded his head. "Yes, so I hear. That will be great for the city. It could do with some injection of culture. Anyway, Erica, thanks for meeting up with me. Didn't want to ask you at the funeral, it seemed inappropriate, but now, well here we are. I have this huge, massive, favour to ask you? And I just know it's going to cost me more than a cheese and onion pizza."

Erica raised her head in the air a little and shook her long, brown hair loose; followed by a long deep sigh. "Ok, Mr Hastings, hit me with it, and before you say anything it will definitely cost you more than just pizza and a quick beer this time."

Hastings removed the vellum clad parchment from his pocket and placed it on the bench; he also removed a single gold Reichsbank 5 mark coin from his pocket and placed it in her hand. "Could you let me know if this coin is from the same batch of coins taken from the lost Deutsche Reichsbank haul, from World War II—Bavaria? You know the Eagle's nest stuff near Berchesgaden or Toplizt. Adolf Hitler and all that tosh, etc. And wads of stolen antiquities. I just happen to know that you had some deposits delivered to your office from a good source last year to authenticate, and I know that you just love this stuff. But that's not all Erica, honest, trust me when I say I think I have found several hundred other gold bars or bullion from the same haul."

Erica was almost stunned as she spun the coin in her fingers, then spoke quietly at first. "Looks authentic enough."

Hastings grabbed the vellum. "It apparently belongs to the Teutonic—Italiano Knights of Palerno." He said no more.

"Kemp, are you shittin me?" she exclaimed, whilst trying to keep her tone at a reasonable level.

"You are such an idiot! You will end up in a heap of trouble just like that bloody Saunier French priest did years ago. This is real blood money, Kemp, people involved with this cache have just fallen off the face of the planet, and these people who want this haul, they don't play cops and robbers, they play shoot you and your bloody dead, now! Here, take your blood tarnished money back!"

She placed the coin back in his hand. Erica was perplexed and very annoyed and carried on with her rabid recital of self-discipline and honesty routine. "At least the Frenchman was clever enough to have backing from the French ministry; a recognized body to deal with any German henchman. But, who is going to protect you when the guns come shooting, eh? No. No. Kemp, please don't do this. Take my advice and run away from this one whilst you still can."

Hasting placed his soft leather gloved hand on top of her hand and squeezed a little. "Shhhh, no, this is not what you think. It's certainly not that bad. I have actually been commissioned by no other than the 'Knights' Templar Order' themselves to conduct an internal audit into what actual inventory they may still hold. I am permitted access to all sorts of places, churches vaults . . . and goodness knows where or what next, and recently these coins have been placed at my disposal. I just need to know if they are authentic that's all. I won't be selling them on eBay or anything like that."

Erica stared backwards and around the immediate vicinity as if she was expecting some kind of a raid to happen momentarily.

"They, the Order, have furnished me with a fair degree of access to both artifacts and people, and these coins, my fair maiden, are legitimate, and I am definitely not on some half arsed cock, adventure treasure trail. This is the real McCoy, Erica, and I am meeting the Grand Prior and Lord Chamberlain later this week to start the internal touchy feely stuff."

Erica lay the coin down and picked up the vellum parchment, she was still a bit uncomfortable, she hated being exposed to anything she had no control over.

"11th century, hand woven and has been well cleaned. It's not pig, it's horse skin, I think. Where did you get this from Kemp? Not the usual vellum of pig skin or cowhide; it is much softer. No, I am sure that this is actually pure horse skin, and it has been deliberately over stretched and look here . . . very thin. Then it has been bonded in some sort of honey and lemon juice after putrefaction."

Hastings clasped his hands. "Here we go with the honey shit again," he muttered, and placed a hand over the vellum, then muttered a few words as Erica shuffled the vellum in her hands.

"I think it may have belonged to a Grand Master of the ancient Knights' Templar Order. I actually shouldn't have it, as its last owner was . . ." he paused, and stared at Erica for approval. She smirked and tilted her head to one side. "The owner apparently died recently and had posted this to me."

Erica began shaking her head again. "Exactly my point, you know what, Kemp Hastings, you are like a bad luck charm—a cosmic tornado wrapped in hog's skin, a shit magnet, and you get the people around you into some serious shitty scrapes. I'll tell you what, I will have a look at this, give me two days or so and I will send you my findings. But for now, don't contact me until I know I am safe. I am not going through another episode of Raiders of the

Lost Ark with you and that's final. I will call you tomorrow, and you can eat your own bloody pizza."

She grabbed her jacket leaving Hastings sitting on the bench to contemplate his next move.

He watched on as the lovely Erica Vine jumped into a taxi and headed up towards the Hill Town district of the city.

Three o'clock the next day, Erica very reluctantly had agreed to meet again with Hastings, although she knew he could be a bit off the cuff, and headstrong, she had a soft spot for him and had pulled out all the stops to appease his current investigation requests, but had assisted him more from her professional capacity as opposed to just being a friend.

She spoke with authority on behalf of the GUE institution. "Now listen, Kemp, the guys worked until two o'clock his morning. I owe them a night out and you are going to pay for it," she said, pointing her pointy finger at him. "Anyway your coins and fishy thing, under lab conditions we use a series of tests that can determine many things. I chose to test under three broad approaches, one of which is a touchstone technique, we normally apply this approach for sensitive and very valuable pieces or softer metals because it is a non-destructive test where only miniscule particles and scrapings from the object are analysed. We also do a second sub-test, or a soft abrasive test: this means rubbing the item across a stone treated with various acids, and then we conduct a colour comparison check."

Hastings was amused; he had never thought about acids and abrasion to inspect works of art. His ignorance, however, did not manifest itself for Miss Vine to exploit.

"We did however find a concentration of 30-45 parts per thousand of gold content as opposed to normal gold calculations which fall normally between 10 or 20 per parts per thousand. This means for this test your wartime booty or this portion of it is made from the purest of gold dating certainly from the mid-16th century. That is only based on colour variation of course."

"Of course," he replied. "And this is your initial diagnosis? Erica, well done. And that's what is known as a touchstone test? I never even knew it existed."

Erica did not detect any condescending tone in his voice and continued. "The second full test we conducted is known as a fluorescence X-ray examination, again a non-destructive test or technique that is used for normal assaying requirements; mainly for flat or relatively flat surfaces. This has an accuracy of approximately 2 to 5 parts per thousand. Here is a copy of the printout."

She placed the printout on the leather glove box between the seats of his car. Hastings quizzed it from a distance, not wishing to appear too eager in his drive for information regarding what was now a rather desirable set of items.

"In essence, Kemp, there is no modern day tampering or fabrication on the coin, it is pure genuine 19th century and can be an expensive item to replace, given its volatile history.'

Hastings placed a finger on the printout. "What is assaying? I mean without getting too complicated please, I only have a little brain," he asked, with genuine interest.

Erica gave him a gentle smile then explained. "Assaying is the process of removing lead or other ores from gold. It is basically a process that employs various techniques to identify the properties of a physical substance, it can be used for silver but it is not as efficient, it is known as critical cupellation or separation method.

To put it into perspective, it is the test used on gold bullion for high purity tests to international standards, but can be narrowed down to parts per million, it is the most accurate appraisal for determining the quality of gold.' Hastings rubbed his chin.

"You and I should get into gold smithing," he said, softly. "And what about the fish?"

Erica smiled. "Extraordinarily. That's almost exactly the same gold quality as your Reichsbank coin, but the fish article appears to have an added substance, we think it is a mixture of stone or . . . crushed bone."

Hasting's eyebrows rose somewhat, leaving an expression of bewilderment on his face.

"I know!" cried Erica. "Isn't that amazing?"

Picking up the printout. He gazed over the numbers and a few completed ticked boxes, then noticed at the bottom of the list was a marking: '99.9 % pure gold quality'. 1000 ppt. In gold terms this was an article that would rival the quality of gold in the British Royal crown jewels.

The only caveat being that a second opinion would be required, just in case Miss Vine had screwed up the testing, but that was quite unlikely for a woman with a PhD in chemistry and an archaeology degree as a side line.

Hastings knew that various processes at the refineries for valuing iron ore or gold would be a good follow up point, but it would be very time consuming, and he really did not wish to second-guess Erica although she was not one hundred percent behind this venture.

"Thank you, Erica, if I plan any trips would you come along for the ride?" he asked, expectant of a very negative answer.

"Why not? You have tried to have me killed already. No point in stopping there now is there?"

CHAPTER FIFTEEN

Custodians

It was two days after his discussion with Erica that Hastings had visited the home of his contact, the late Dr Niven Airlie—his name provided by his employer in order to conduct some routine audit questioning. The meeting now almost a figment of Hasting's fertile mind.

Hastings removed his little black book from his laptop bag and started to re-read some of his accounts and had jotted down some points that the late Dr Niven had passed on to him.

Hastings in his mind's eye walked his way back in time and retraced the day's events thoroughly in his head.

Doctor Norman Niven Airlie, had answered the door and made him more than welcome and provided him with a nice hot cup of tea, then, they both spent some time wandering through the Doctor's humble abode, albeit, according to his notes the house was something more that resembled a ram shackled museum than an actual dwelling house.

Hastings recalled that Dr Niven was the current Templar custodian of several hundred artifacts that the order had entrusted into his care, and was obviously more concerned about his own health and wanted to ensure himself that he was capable of remaining as a custodian, albeit, the audit was also a good opportunity and excuse to give Hastings the once over.

Amongst the clutter of this biblical horde, Hastings had taken time to touch as much of the Holy relics as possible. What caught his immediate attention back then, were a clutch of 11th or 12th century wooden caskets, a series of five boxes that were stacked up in no particular order in one of the corners of the room.

One box in particular had caught his prying eye, and he instantly recognized it as an American George Washington Benevolent pine desk casket, the box sat with its ornate lid in the open position exposing the interior.

The inside of the coffer was very well decorated and was lined with a light honey, brown oak veneer, and housed an internal set of two drawers which were closed and had been sealed with a small Templar chain seal.

The adjoining pigeon holes held a range of different sized parchments and documents and some very old looking scrolls that appeared to have been semi-stuffed into the many recesses. Hastings thought at that time a bit bizarre considering they were serious antique documents, and left out for all to see, as he recalled, and had flicked his fingers gingerly over a few pages of a brown vellum manuscript. "Verdi," he had muttered, then had asked a series of questions.

His first question? Was, 'Nice collection you have here Doctor?" he said again softly, taking time to almost deliberately touch a larger box with his right knee. The Doctor remained silent and watched with interest. The box was almost like a British Army Officer's war chest, but this chest was somewhat more ornate and was adorned with a square edged vaulted lid.

The locking mechanism was easily older than 15th century and consisted of two steel plates that overwrapped the lid area and stretched down the spine and backing panel of the body, an elegant arch shape to form a hinge and bolt type coffer.

The external decoration was quite exquisite and very elegant and had been formed from several layers of thin veneer of ivory and mother of pearl which had been neatly inlaid to the larger oak paneling across the four major panels with acute precision, each seam was perfect.

Hastings remembered vividly glancing back at the table top box and spied a small picture of George Washington neatly placed between two indented information slots on the flat surface, the photograph itself was of good quality and had been placed behind a single glass panel of which, the initials of the previous owner, A.M. 1144 KT sat either side of the glass.

Niven had looked up and spoke. "We have many relics to manage in here, far too many for me alone. Sometimes, I think that I should sell the lot and run away off to Barbados or somewhere hot like that or a location as equally as warm with a sandy beach, I would . . ." he then laughed a little.

"If I had the younger legs and a more fertile mind and of course the inclination to, I would have run away to some obscure island," he muttered again, then started laughing out loudly.

"Luckily for us, young Mr Hastings, the Order would only come looking for me, and claim it all back, believe me young man, when I say that there is nowhere to run and certainly nowhere to hide from the Order, because the mighty clandestine fighting machine has eyes and ears everywhere."

Hastings had been in agreement and had nodded his head accordingly, then moved nonchalantly toward a large oak desk nearer toward the bay window recess, then posed a single question. "Tell me, Doctor Niven? How do you know what actual artifacts you have in your possession? I mean look at this place, it is littered with relics, boxes and things of special interest, if it was located anywhere else we would call it a museum," he asked, searching for any indications of lists or records.

"I mean, it must be difficult to see what you actually have in this room alone, but how do you or the Order for example, know what is contained in all those other boxes or cupboards? Or conversely, if the Knights' Templar Order actually still own great amounts of wealth ranging from fortresses, castles, churches, vaults cathedrals, livestock, etc., then how does the Grand Master know where it is all physically kept? And by whom? Or where?"

Hastings recalled cutting the question short, and had stared at the old man directly, and was expectant of a comprehensive answer, and as expected, an answer of sorts eventually came. "Three questions posed collectively in one good question, Mr Hastings, but . . . well, that's the real mystery isn't it? We, as an Order, probably really don't know ourselves where everything is kept,

I mean a great deal was stolen, there have been events such as fires and acts of theft and simple banter, day to day swapping, and it is as simple as that. So, if you are searching for a comprehensive inventory of the Holy Relics or a single record of armour and riches, then I am sorry that I am going to have to disappoint you young man."

The Doctor had then wandered out the room and into another room, Hastings followed like all good puppy dogs should, especially when being escorted around such a worldly place, then stopped by the tall Scottish Grandfather clock. Hastings recalled the time: 33 minutes past the hour of midnight or mid-day, depending on how your melatonin levels are working out, and this clock strikes thirteen at midnight.

"You see, there is only one person at any one time who holds the 'Templari Thesaurus' secrets, or knows of its exact location, and that my dear friend will be the Grand Master himself. But even then, if he or she is in a vulnerable employment position, say a soldier or a sailor as an example, then there is the adage of a designated pseudo custodian or: 'alter ego' to contemplate. This 'alter ego' will be another designated person who retains the whereabouts of the parchment itself, but may never actually see the article up close and comfy, he or she will just be informed of the documents whereabouts by the Grand Master.

It's all very complex and intriguing how the Order actually manages business, Mr Hastings, and I suppose, it would not be of any surprise to you to know that only four 'alter ego' custodians in our tainted past have been put to the sword as a result of their greed and deception. If you study the rule of the rule, or the guidance of the order, this item of deceit falls under—the header of theft or—rule 246 or even rule 250 and prior to any judgment the Knights would have been placed in 'irons' then most likely derobed, or their habit removed, then perhaps, flogged, but, in certain cases corporal punishment and capital punishment was not all that uncommon.

Well, not too recently, I may hasten to add, but over the past three centuries or so, each in their own mad cap campaign or personal crusade to relieve the Order of its many riches. The last 'alter ego' dispatched to God by the Order was a Knight and Scribe called William De Souza the 3rd, circa August 1840, just before the French rebellion had physically kicked off again.

He and an accomplice played their particular tune in harmony with a foreign violin along with one Napoleon Bonaparte, and they both paid very dearly. Historical records will never show us, but internal Templar execution documents will tell the reader exactly what happened. Each man slaughtered by the blade of the 'Whispering Swordsman, or perhaps a Swordswoman. We must be politically correct these days, one can't always tell what the Order is thinking, they just move stealthily and silently through history ducking and diving at all times whilst keeping control of those who need controlling."

Hastings pursed his lips again then nodded; he had recalled his response to the Dr's warning statement, then had commented, "Dodgy business indeed. One can't go around selling the family silver now can we? Anyway, the real reason why I am here, Pastor, is that I have called in on you to ask a few questions regarding The Knights' Templar Order. And to ask how they work the inventory process? This question is required for me to close out an audit item on my vast list of things to locate and record."

Had he memorized the complete conversation, yes he had and then ran it and back through his head word for word: "What I am looking for is details of the merging of equal Orders from SMOTJ to OSMTH in 1985 or 1995. And although I can find general information of where and when it occurred, I can find no real time documentation to indicate who was designated or who assumed the duties of the overarching Grand Master and what inventory controls were put in order to merge the ledgers. My reasons for this request are quite plain, you see, I have been tasked to specifically audit what I tangibly can for the Order, but it is quite difficult when all of the relevant information or articles are not so readily available."

The old vicar took a deep breath and placed a scrawny, aged hand on a small table top box—an item that Hastings had somehow missed during his initial scanning of the many relics in the room; a very ornate box that was sitting almost obscured amongst a plethora of other bits and bobs on the large Victorian drawer set.

The Pastor had slowly opened the box and removed three pieces of paper and a small book from the casket. Hasting's eyes widened as he spied the book; a book which had been written on the subject of medieval armour which now sat within the vicar's frail, old hand and was at this moment in time Mr Hastings's 'not' so favourite read, remaining mindful of his German pursuers.

Hastings remembering being somewhat on edge as the old man shot him a rather extraordinary look as if he knew somehow, that he may have had an inclination as to the significance of the pages.

But Hasting had controlled his desire to just grab the book, slap the old man and flee out of the house in all haste. However, that was the pivotal moment when the 'clerk of God' began to speak with a more reverend and somewhat more controlled softer tone.

A question came back from the cleric in response.

"Do you know much about medieval armour, Mr Hastings?" whilst he was in the process of removing an inner leaf page from within the book he held in his hands. Hastings tilted his head back slightly forwards then responded.

"Only what I have read in journals, books and by watching Ivanhoe and William Tell on the television, but I did see one of those big blockbuster movies, Gladiator with Russell thingy, you know the dark haired actor," he said, whilst smiling very nonchalantly at the old cleric. The old man tapped the top of the box.

"Mmmh! Well, this Mr Hastings, this little chap here is a hand crafted piece of Siculo—Arabic wood—which was formed into this casket at least 745 years ago. It was probably made some time after the era that your actor chappy, Mr Russell Crow the Gladiator, who played the part of Markus Aurilious or whatever his name was in the epic film.

The box itself was made in the year 1131 by Chevalier William Irons, a master carpenter and the best in class for his time, and by all accounts was a Scottish settler in the holy land. He was accompanied by a young squire apprentice or carpenter's assistant, who executed the fine internal display and immaculate inlay of the box you see before you. He could have been his son or nephew. I don't know I am not that old," he said, and smiled.

The old man explained further whilst pointing toward the red silken lining in the case. "But this young man was also the squire to the great and ubiquitous Hugues De Payens himself and that was not an easy honour to have bestowed up on you, Mr Hastings.

Oh no! This young chap must have been an excellent scholar and master craftsman, and a student who showed signs of great promise, but of course that was back in those days, long gone by and most probably drowned in the sands of time. If we could believe all history today, Mr Hastings, and I think we should believe most of it, you may just be able to trace the lineage of those master tradesman straight back to their front doors, but only if you know where to look.

And if you search hard and long enough, it is amazing what revelations come to light. Would you like another cup of tea?" he asked, then scratched his scraggily brow. Hastings had stared back toward the box. He could now see why it was easily 12th century and did indeed support a well-tailored red linen interior; by his reckoning Hastings surmised it was the original hand crafted work.

In his mental recall and muddled ramblings he recalled the boxes and the conversation he had with the old man, and the mood of the old man, it was all rather too complex for him to fit into his little brain. He read through his notes again.

The exterior of the wee box however, was something completely different and was coated in fine almost white enamel ivory veneers, the outer panels were adorned with crudely etched peacocks and camels, coupled with a range of fauna entwined with flora motifs and a few fleur de lis etchings, that had been delicately coloured and applied after the meticulous and careful carving had been complete.

The box had a series of letters carved across the outer part of the lid. They simply read: HdeP-GM, either side of the name a carved rose. The old man had paused and placed the book on the small 15th century Japanese coffee table.

"Yes, Mr Hastings, it is what you think it is! That box once belonged to the founding Grand Master himself, and of which has been passed down through the Order's ranks and up through the centuries until now, and I have the honor and glory of being its current custodian. Imagine what secrets it could tell. But after all is said and done, it is still only a box, it might be worth a few quid or several sheckles to the right collector, but it's secrets, well, they are something entirely different. If this little piece of ivory could talk, what would it say?

I think the stories would not only be unbelievable and perhaps this wee box has witnessed information that may have changed the course of history itself. But what about the Order as stories and mysterious rumblings that ran rife within the Order, stories telling of treasure trails that could lead a person to great wealth that was simply un-measureable."

Hastings pursed his lips again, as he read the footnotes and conversation questions he had recorded in his little black book. He remembered vividly asking the Doctor a few questions.

"Dr Niven, why are you telling me all this? Surely the hierarchy of the Order must have vows of secrecy and silence concerning such details. I mean who could imagine someone trying to sell the Order's family silver as it were on the Internet or at a car boot sale, or in the papers perhaps. Is it public knowledge that this is what the Order does?"

Hastings had laughed out loud and so had the old man; probably one of the last laughs the old man had before dying. Hasting went through their conversation again piece by piece word by word.

"No, no, Mr Hastings, as I have said before, the Order only release information that they want released, you have a wise old head on a very young pair of shoulders and you of all people must know that the Order does not do things straight off the cuff or on the spur of a moment.

Everything they do, right down to the most miniscule of detail is thoroughly thought through and executed with anticipated outcomes. And they do sell artifacts and modern day trinkets in Malta or Mdina or Roslin, it is all part of the modern day economics of the Order. That's why you are here, working under the premise that the Fisher Kings sent you on a Queen's or King's errand: a task to conduct an archival internal audit on behalf of the Holy Order, and to find out more about the 'Templari Thesaurus' inventory was that not correct? Well, my dear Brother Hastings, there it is over there," he said, pointing to the boundary wall of the Priory.

The investigator leaned toward the window and stared out. "What are we talking about? Is it the wall or the actual graves themselves, Doctor?" he retorted, and still somewhat confused, but harbouring the notion that the wall might have some rather interesting mason marks or symbols etched into its stony surface.

"No, Mr Hastings, not the wall and not the graves, but the windows of the Kirk. They are there for all to see, but it's what you don't see that matters."

Hastings was desperate to latch on to the unclear clues the old man was laying out before him, but he could not grasp things fully until the old man said the magic word 'illumination'.

Kemp Hastings closed his little book and thought very hard about the conversation regarding the actual manuscripts. Niven had been very clear when he explained what was there for all to see. Hastings recalled his actual words: 'When we see the light of day, things become less vague. Now this book on medieval armour is a sort of an illuminated manuscript. There are several others of these parchments in existence and not every Templar is furnished with one. I know that you don't have your copy yet, because I hear you missed conclave two months ago, so, I will have to give you my copy as a token gesture.

One must remain mindful that there is always only one grand master copy that contains a concise list of very important names. However, every Templar knows that the contemporary approved copy must never see the light of modern day, until succession has occurred.' There had been another one of those really awkward silence moments between the two men. Hastings knew he had missed the last three gatherings over the past year, but had diligently paid his oblations during his absence. And how did the old man know anyway?

He promised himself that he would make every effort to attend next conclave in a month or so, but somehow he thought it may well be irrelevant if the Order was already setting him up for a mighty fall or something far greater.

The cleric had also placed that book in his hand. "This is the third book of medieval armour. It is rumored that one copy, as I have already stated is in circulation, and contains the elusive 'Templari Thesaurus'. There are, I think, only 'nine' historical copies in total of this rather unique 'Scottish' inventory which have been produced, and then again, another single special copy has the secret codex embedded within its informative pages. Information that reveals the true resting place of the 'master ledger', this is the ledger that contains all."

Hastings recalled as the old man picked up a document and was reading through its many pages as they spoke, as if he was indicating something.

"It is rumoured that the Pope himself had previously signed the older ledgers in his tenure as pontiff, but after the year 1742, the Vatican left the duty of reconciliation to the Grand Masters, And now, Mr Hastings, those ledgers require updating and that is where you and the two lovely ladies can assist us."

Hastings was suddenly flummoxed. He had the feeling as if he had been played for the fool for the past four months, especially more so being hired to conduct a series of investigations on behalf of the Fisher King and The Knights' Templar Order, or where they just many fabricated shenanigans and antics to test his mettle.

But as a Knight himself of the RL (Royal Lodge), he played the role and conducted himself just as the Order had anticipated. He did not exactly feel used but more relieved to know, now that the Order would also protect him, and of course Madelyn and Erica.

He opened the now interesting book on armour at the front page. Then flicked through the first five pages. He flicked the book over to find the initials, F.R. embossed in gold on the leather, inside cover, and had cracked, what he thought, would be a simple joke but the old cleric obviously had been given a sense of humour 'bypass' at some stage of his life.

"You will be telling me next that this book belonged to Francis Robert, St Clair Erskine, the renowned gentlemen and socialite and 4th Earl of Roslin, the man who had deliberately secreted half the temple's so called wealth under the Chapel then filled it in with tons upon tons of sand to keep it safe. Incidentally, exactly the same process as they would have conducted within an ancient pyramid funerary ritual. I think he died about 1890 or thereabouts, obviously liked the sandy beaches," retorted Hastings.

The old man smirked. "You are not too far off the beaten track young man. I will say that much for you. The 4th Earl, however, did have some rather extreme ideas, but they were all executed in the preservation of what the Temple holds in the highest esteem. And, if you were able to cast your mind back in time to the early 1840's, you would find that life was very different back then. But today is where we are. We need to prepare you for your future custodial duties."

Hastings stopped and stared at the cleric. "My what!" he exclaimed, taking time to ensure he had heard the old buzzard correctly. That was the first real inclination that Kemp Hastings knew he had been singled out for some role or other, but he struggled with the concept of more work, as he enjoyed his investigative life.

"My dear Mr Hastings, you are fifteen years plus as a Knight in the Templar organisation, and you have probably missed most of our gatherings, but in your capacity as envoy to the Fisher Kings and indeed our Order, you have, my dear young man, achieved the right to become a steward of Scotland.

I am merely an old Lord Chamberlain and Chief archivist but thirty years ago, I was a former member of the elite Swiss Guard in the Vatican City you know, and that honor was bestowed upon me through my grandfather's rights. We must ensure that the family silver and lineage is always kept safe, I am sure you can understand that."

Hasting sat down and contemplated his position. He knew he did not want to refuse any requests by the Knights' Order and he knew at some point he would have to support the Order from within. And this was perhaps his calling, a cry for his duty, to be placed before all other things, and he readily agreed to take custody of his inventory.

"So what do I have to do?" he asked, clasping his hands.

The old priest then wiped his brow and gave a small cough. "Not a great deal really. I suppose you have already received a parcel in the post from somewhere recently; something similar to that little booklet we have there. And I assume you have secreted it somewhere safe? Perhaps in a tree, or in a nice shiny box like this one here, or you may have even hidden the document in a grave perhaps, maybe an upturned grave stone in Mary Kirk, or more importantly you might have actually found the resting place of the Green Man?"

Hastings was awestruck. He would have never imagined, in a million years, that he could have been that predictable—he was bloody annoyed to say the very least.

"Oh, don't worry, Mr Hastings, the Grand Master's 'Templari Thesaurus' has never left Malta, I can assure you of that. What you have is the associated cipher codes; a list of dates and locations," said the old man, clasping his hands together. "It is guarded by no less than three 'squires' at any one time and has probably never even seen the light of day since the year 1735."

That was when Hastings rubbed his brow and lowered his head, and reached forward for his cup of tea, then explained some new developments to the cleric. Hastings recalled that old vicar was a bit displaced by the new revelation.

"Ah, well, Doctor Airlie, if that is the case then I think, that I may have some rather disturbing news to offer you, you see during World War II, I understand that the Grand Master's 'Templar Thesaurus' was moved," he said, whilst inverting his fingers high in the air. "Le dossier und das importanti buch or your inventory book, in fact, the one on 'medieval armour' was somehow placed together along with a clutch of other library books and documents that were literally dumped into a box aptly marked 'The art of warfare'. A single book like the very one you have there was inadvertently also enclosed within the batch, or it may have been placed there deliberately. I mean, who knows?

What were the chances of the codex and the Thesaurus being co-located in one country? Maybe, a million to one? The consignment of mixed literature was then sent across middle Europe, only to end up twenty-three miles away across the motorway at Restenneth Priory. A token donation for the Angus archives to pass on to a local charity shop. The 'Templari Thesaurus' and the wee book of armour has come all the way from Acre or Temple Mount in the Holy land to borderland, Germany Malta and now Scotland. Of course, however in its incredible journey from Acre it apparently ended up in middle Switzerland at some point, for quite some time around the mid 1940's.

It was then recorded for disposal or sent to a smaller church nearer the Swiss, Bavarian border lands, where it remained for about eight months or so when it was intercepted by a Nazi war machine special task force, who were after something completely different during a daring World War II raid. And was therefore, caught up in the melee as part of project Avalon.

So, to cut a very long and complicated story very short, the consignment eventually made its way here to bonnie Scotland, and I have it secreted away from unscrupulous treasure seekers who know a fair bit of what is going on."

The investigator clearly remembered the old man's reaction as the priest laughed out loud and burbled whilst shaking his head in disbelief. "You believe all those coincidences have actually naturally occurred do you? A secret book hidden from prying eyes, then it was really misfiled, then sent to yet another foreign country. Then somehow, became part of some wartime Avalonian operational plot in World War II, and, as a penultimate measure, was then eventually recovered from Switzerland only to be sent to Scotland. Well, Mr Hastings you should be writing science fiction stories instead of investigating them—that's far too bizarre to believe."

Hastings had placed his tea cup on the saucer and gave the subject matter a bit more thought. He had quizzed another parchment that day; it was a letter that lay on the table top—it read: News brief—dated 1994, secret tunnels discovered under the streets of Acre, main tunnel entrance discovered. 1000 feet long terminates at Khan al Shuna.

Hastings felt for the parchment in his inner pocket and found the dossier, it was still safe. He knew when he had returned to retrieve the document from the grave of the 'Green Man' that someone would be watching, and he would be correct in this assumption, but the person watching him was not a German or a guardian Knight, it was a Dame of the new world Order.

The grave had not been touched or disturbed and was just as he had left it, when he arrived to recover the 'Templari Thesaurus'. The only difference was that it was not raining and a single black crow was sitting on the gravestone.

When he approached the site, it was approximately five o'clock in the morning, and again, whilst working under the cloak of darkness, his partner Doctor Madelyn Linn who was also in attendance, not only to witness the recovery of the document, but to stamp her seal of approval on the antics of Kemp Hastings on behalf of the Order.

His conversation and meeting with the old man was a meeting that he was unlikely to forget. He made a few other notes in his little black book, and made his way to his car.

CHAPTER SIXTEEN

Medieval Armour

The Grand Master's Armour

B ack in his flat, Hastings picked up the book on medieval armour from the table top and quizzed its very plain and boring dust cover. The protective sheet itself comprised of a close fitting vellum parchment with a thin piece of twisted leather strapping which had been ripped, but pretty much held the spine in place.

The main body of the book originally held 42 pages, of which had 5 pages had either been removed or torn from the work.

Page 32, was quite a simple page but ironically the adjacent page was not page 33 but two blank pages: where Page 32 and 33 should have been, but were deliberately printed on the out facing page. It was as if this book was printed with the application of an envelope being the intention and made deliberately on purpose to house what we now know is the 'Di Templari Thesaurus'.

The page explained that 'A Knight's Armour' was for more than just protection of his warring lifestyle but resonated the Knight's actual rank or status within the military Order. The more ornate and the more gold it was adorned with, the more it would signify a high ranking official's nobility or official status, and would certainly have pointed clearly in the direction towards the social elite class of the day.

Full body fighting armour is expensive and a major piece of capital investment for both the Knight and the Order and the many Grand Masters wore it with great pride, albeit not many died in battle wearing this style of attire.

Hastings began to see how the management of armour and the subtle physical changes would affect personal warfare, but he somehow could not grasp the reason why the Grand Master had chosen a book on 'armour' to hide the most expensive shopping list in the history of mankind within its pages.

The not so well known fact about armour is that some of the more elite costumes are made of a thin gold plate which was donned by the Grand Masters and came in at an extraordinary weight of almost 20 kilograms of plated gold. The gold complimented the suit as a splattering of ornate plates and pins.

By today's bullion market prices, one kilogram of gold bullion would cost approximately £34,000 per ingot or bullion bar, and if a full sized armour suit was made, then the cost in today's market would class and ledger the armour as a 'major capital asset' in any major corporation.

The Grand Order of the Temple can boast 36+ such suits of armour, and of which a range can be located in the Cathedral in Mdina, Malta and other locations dotted over the globe. Hastings reflected back to a recent visit to Malta and paused for thought.

"God in heaven above!" he exclaimed. "Today that would cost almost £6.8 million, each, and of course with 36 of them to account for, that was almost something like £244.8 million bucks!" Hastings was astounded as the enormity of a single cost of armour hit home. Of course, by comparison the cost of armour in the year 1127 was much cheaper but nevertheless still a substantial outlay for the order even back then.

He carried reading the full contents of the now very interesting book on war armour and sat back in the comfy chair with a warm brandy and sighed. After a few minutes, he looked back over the book and momentarily picked up an oddity of where the lettering on one of the pages was either thicker or had been at some point printed in a bolder script.

He thought about De Payens flicking through the pages and was hopeful for an example of his handwriting or at best his signature.

'First Indicator—Armour almanac 1119'.

> *Knot or loop arrangement was used which sometimes hung from the shoulder. The breast—and back-plates would be attached on one side with short loops of cord acting as a hinge,* and *on the other by a longer and more ornate tied one (as with boots, the longer the lace, the less the need to undo the entire lace). As armour became* more *ornamental and moved away from basic design, becoming less standard and practical, so too did the ties. This explains the aiguillettes of varying levels of complexity in the uniforms of the British Household Cavalry, (as opposed to other regiments that have never been armoured). Extract page 31, definition De Payens H.*

Hastings photocopied the page then traced the bold lettering whilst highlighting the wording with a blue pen. A few moments later, he paused and tried to make sense of the writing. Then he realised how close he was to touching actual history. The bold lettering simply read: KT Andre' Montbard.

Hastings knew, at this moment, Hugues De Payens had already marked Andre Montbard as his successor as Grand Master at some point in his Templar life, and that the book in question on 'armour' was not anywhere near 14th century but could have been in existence as early as the 12th century. And, after careful scrutiny, was littered with many words being over typed or written in bold throughout the script.

The investigator had stumbled on something almost amazing and wrote down the complete book with all the bold letters highlighted. He also noticed that all of the writing was placed on the 'even' numbered pages from 4, through to 8, 12, 14, 18, 20, 24, 30, 32, 36, 40, 44, 48 and 50.

Passing the mantle of succession was not an easy task for any Grand Master to consider, and a great deal of amount of psychological profiling was necessary to ensure the right man for the job was chosen, and sufficient time was available to coach and mentor the successor into the line of succession—which was absolutely crucial.

In the case of Andre Montbard, this would have been an easy decision for De Payens to make as Montbard had spent several years on the killing fields, as it were, fighting side by side with the evolving Grand Master.

His allegiance to Hugues De Payens would have been unwavering as they had formed the Order on an equal footing. Andre' may not have possessed De Payen's political or business acumen or was an active member of the upper classes, but he clearly had the knowledge and the ability and the serious connections to keep the Order stable and free and out of harm's way when it was required.

In his tenure, Montbard, (1153-1156) had laid the foundation stones of building the careers of many squires and servants who served their Knights, but were almost inextricably linked to The Knights' Templar as soon as they were procured to serve the order.

Often was the case that squires would act as alter egos for thirty six months and would often sit in the saddle of their peers as a precaution prior to becoming a postulant or trainee Knight.

As the mechanics of the Order functioned silently in the background, Andre' Montbard would learn of his courtship by the Grand Master by a series of engagements; whereupon being the GM 'alter ego' (GM ae). He would stand in as a representative and slowly, but surely, learn the protocols of mastery. A rule within a rule to run business.

The final stage of the selection process would be a test of character, followed by a few simple but relevant tasks to test the mettle of the Knight by exposure to voluptuous females—exposure to riches and finally exposure to integrity and honesty.

Each stage would be managed by the Grand Master himself, and one of which were judgements based on everyday life. On several occasions, the 'alter ego' would attend fiscal ceremonies and play a part in judgements, for the betterment of the order.

Hasting reached into his leather satchel and removed a single copy letter of the Order's Statutes, he was more interested in the format of the text block more than anything else, and often used this template to authenticate other existing Templar documentation.

He placed the two documents together on the wooden Mexican coffee table and quizzed their content. He was searching for two distinct symbols and signatures and found them embedded on the Les Statuts Généraux—1705 A.D./The General Statutes—1705 A.D and the

ORDRE   DU TEMPLE,

STATUTS

DES CHEVALIERS DE L'ORDRE DU TEMPLE,

FORMÉS DES RÈGLES SANCTIONNÉES DANS LES CONVENTS-GÉNÉRAUX
ET RÉDIGÉS EN UN SEUL CODE,
PAR LE CONVENT-GÉNÉRAL DE VERSAILLES, L'AN 586 (1705).

A. M. D. G.

PHILIPPE, Grand-Maître de la Milice du Temple; Jean-Hercule d'Afrique, Lieutenant-Général; François-Louis-Léopold d'Europe, Lieutenant-Général; Marie-Louis
d'Amérique, Lieutenant-Général; Henri d'Asie, Lieutenant-Général,

Par la grâce de Dieu et les suffrages de Nos Frères, Princes Souverains de
l'Ordre,

A tous ceux qui ces présentes verront, SALUT, SALUT, SALUT.

Le Convent-Général des Chevaliers du Temple, tenu à Versailles, le vingt-neuf de
la Lune d'Adar, l'an de l'Ordre, cinq cent quatre-vingt-six, a réuni les présentes Règles
pour en former les Statuts de l'Ordre.

CHAPTER SEVENTEEN

Temple Dust

The Learjet aeroplane touched down at Sion . . . Switzerland's airport, at 07:28 hours. The landing was soft and smooth and executed by the Swiss National Red Cross pilot Bernard De Silvio; a pilot with twenty years of service to the Swiss National Order.

The private charter air program, operated within the Order, had delivered Kemp Hastings, Erica Vine and Madelyn Linn into Switzerland without any undue fuss, before the trio even stepped off the plane and onto the cold, grey tarmac. They had already cleared customs and were being picked up by a host driver and were to be driven to Andermatt some 120 kilometres away.

As she stepped off the small, steel stairway, Erica smiled as the big, black Range Rover slowly pulled up alongside the jet and she glanced back at Madelyn with a grin that resembled the 'cat got the cream' type of smirk.

Madelyn responded pretty much the same way, as Hasting stood and watched on as the pair unceremoniously shuffled their way into the rear of the car and waited for him to grab their soft luggage. He just smiled again.

Within twelve minutes of landing, the 4x4 vehicle was heading eastwards towards the beautiful mountain backdrop that only Switzerland could offer. Hastings had explained to the girls about the last three days events and was busy unfolding a small map page that he had ripped out of his AA traveller's manual.

"Well, ladies we are travelling from here to here," he said, pointing to the red ink pen line that he had feverishly scribbled whilst sitting on the jet.

Erica quickly offered an answer, "The San Gothard—Furka Pass—in this valley connects with the cantons of Uri or the north, and the Ticino."

"South," Hastings smiled and nodded. "Yes, but the pass itself were dug out, east to west, and lies between here and here, and is very important?"

He then traced the line on the map.

"There is a rumour about a 'Devil's Bridge' that lies at the bottom of the Furka Pass. And, from what I can gather, the story is reflected across European history in many shapes and forms—of course that is as far as interesting bridges are concerned. But, what interests me is that the Devil's Bridge was constructed near to the St Bernard's Pass, or what is now locally known as the San Bernardino. Let me say, when I was here thirty odd years ago, we, as a team, jogged up and down this mountain roadway at least twice a week. And, if you think that you have never heard of this pass, or don't think you know it, well, you actually might have seen the long, winding roadway on one of the James Bond films.

The secret, British spy movie being: 'On Her Majesty's Secret Service'. An early film, I grant you, but the car chase up and down this valley was awesome. However, the road is still a killer and bears witness to several accidents per year. But the double bridges here, well, they are more interesting to know about. The Devil's Bridge has probably killed more people than the mountain roadway.

Why? Well, because just as the legend says: 'That when the bridge was finished, the Devil himself was to be paid for permitting any crossings to be undertaken and declared that he wanted the first soul across the bridge as payment'—to this end the people sent a single mountain goat across the bridge as payment, understandably, the devil was not impressed and was severely pissed off and cast a nasty horrible spell for all time over the construction.

The original bridge was known locally as the 'Teufelsbrucke' over the River Reuss and built under many engineering challenges, along with many other bridges in the region, but this bridge actually suffered a more than average amount of drownings and fatalities over the years, and history along with the diabolo influence was forged in legend.

The people back then as a general reaction just simply built a 'new second bridge' across the river Ruess, but today, that is why we observe two bridges offering a choice of crossings.

The legend also says that the herdsman, before the construction, found the crossing so difficult to ford the river that he asked the 'devil', of all entities, for a bridge to be built. Of course, having been duped on other occasions, the devil always reacted with the intention of destroying all bridges if he was betrayed. And this time, after being conned by yet another shepherd or goats man, he was really pissed.

But, earlier in the week, after the bridge was completed, an old, wise lay woman had 'marked' the bridge with a holy cross, and the devil was duped yet again. The huge cross can still be seen above the older bridge cut deep into the rock face, it is approximately 220 tons of solid hard core rock, we will see it in about half an hour or so.

But, now my dear ladies, are you familiar with the great Da Vinci, or his Mona Lisa painting? Of course you are! But did you know that the very same type of devil's arched bridge was also painted on this wonderful painting in the lower left hand corner?

And this enchanted tale must have sat among Leonardo's innermost thoughts also, and again if we went to visit Royal Deeside or Braemar in Scotland, as further examples you will find an exact copy of another Devil's Bridge with, yep, you guessed it! Exactly the same storyline, but, there are of course seven bridges of concern in our belief systems and one of those bridges is reported to lead into to the afterlife."

The trio eventually arrived at their hotel, having viewed the great gorge and observed the Devil's Bridge and its great rock cross, and they agreed the day had been a long one. They decided to take it easy for now, and visit the churchyard early the next day.

After a somewhat restless sleep, Hastings eventually awoke from his sleep pondering on the upcoming events and what adventures lay ahead of them for that day. He thought clearly about where the cemetery was located, and whether or not he should have contacted the Order prior to meeting with Erica and Madelyn, before departing Scotland. He decided to text his new best friend, Colonel Marquis.

Therefore, after a nice Swiss, healthy breakfast of fresh bread and butter sandwiches coated with honey, and a hot coffee, Hastings thought breakfast was the best ever as he was accompanied by the two girls. After which they slowly sauntered up through the rural Swiss village in the crispness of the morning air, and soon found themselves entering the heavy gothic set of gates that served the entrance to the once pseudo wartime cemetery.

They then walked aimlessly through the surprisingly larger graveyard, only stopping now and then to read off some the names that had been carved into the ornate mason work and view the abundance of flowers and trinkets.

They soon found that each grave had been affixed with a small, white porcelain picture of the interred person, and of which, was washed frequently by the old ladies of the village as a mark of their respect.

Erica was clearly disturbed as she spied the graves with dead children's faces staring back at her. And Madelyn, well, she just kept looking behind her as if something was distracting her attentions as opposed to viewing the record of death. Hastings had wandered off to the older part of the bone yard and was leaning over the end gravestone trying to decipher some of the many the lairs identification marks.

Meanwhile, a single muffled pistol shot rang out across the churchyard in front of both Erica and Madelyn they both suddenly stared at one another as the pellet whizzed by, instantly freezing in their footsteps as a second "shot' hit the nearby gravestone sending small, chunky chips of stonework in all directions.

"Shit, that's real gun fire, c'mon let us get the f . . . out of here!" cried Madelyn, as she grabbed Erica's hand and fled into the open doorway of the chapel.

Then quickly the two girls closed the huge door and made their way to the farthest point from the doorway, then hid strategically down behind a large set of wooden pews.

Hastings was oblivious to what was going on just a hundred yards or so away. He was busy scraping the green moss from a gravestone that had been lodged up against the low curtain wall. His concentration was geared to what lay under the earth of Bernard's Swiss plot.

The wind had cancelled out the low muffled report from the pistol as the silencer that was fitted to the handgun did its job, muffled even more by the constant blowing of the wind.

The chapel door opened up slightly then closed again. It was as if the door was being closed from the outside with intent to be secured, and then a fairly loud 'klunk' could be heard clearly within the church as the echoes of the steel mechanism fell into place.

The house of God was momentarily in darkness, less for only a few sprinkles of light from the morning sun's rays—a colourful spread—which was reflected across the altar wall. The two girls stood up in unison, then walked gingerly across the nave and found the eastern vaulted recess and waited. After a few minutes, Erica plucked up enough courage and tried to open the door, but found it had indeed been locked.

Erica stared at the back wall of the altar and watched eagerly as the image of blue apples slowly appeared on the ornate woodwork, just as the sun said good morning in all its glory to the world of cheese and 'the sound of music', albeit the Von Trapp family were nowhere to be seen.

She traced her hands along the wooden slats then suddenly pushed the two central panels inwards, she was acting as if she knew or had anticipated exactly what was going to happen.

"What are you doing?" asked Madelyn, who was watching her every move and was flirting her gaze between Erica and the huge oak wood door, just in case the assailant tried to shoot at them again. Madelyn swore she could hear footsteps in the gravel outside and moved closer towards Erica.

After a few moments of pushing the ornate wooden tongue and groove panelling, two specific panels gave way and slid across to one side of the planking, as the priests bolt hole lay open and exposed.

"I knew this would be here. Kemp will have to find us. He is a big boy; I am sure he will be wondering where we are," said Erica, wiping her hands and staring back at Madelyn.

"You can wait here for Kemp to rescue you, or you could wait until that madman comes back and shoots you dead. But I do not intend dying in a bloody church—let alone a foreign one."

After a few awkward exchanges of facial expressions, the girls had entered the bolt hole and were making their way within the subterranean walls of St John's Chapel, Andermatt.

As Erica Vine and Madelyn Linn made their way through the many caverns and crannies within the church vaults, they could both sense that something was not quite right; a silent hum resonated within the walls and could be heard more loudly in the adjacent chambers.

It was as if a huge generator was pulsing away sending volts upon volts of electricity to the national grid, it was if two corridors ran in parallel but heading in the same direction and the hum was being directed somewhere. Erica spied a series of small lights which darted in and around the large doorway ahead.

She stopped momentarily and began fumbling about in her clutch handbag, a few seconds later she was holding a small, black Maglite torch.

"Don't panic, Maddy. It's just the Girl Guide in me: always like to be prepared for the unknown."

Madelyn cast her an awkward but warm smile as if it say, 'Wow! What else do you have in there lady? A machine gun?'

The two walked on a little further to the next set of archways. Then paused just before entering the dimly lit longer and higher chamber, a single point where all the arches spread outwards and upwards into a more substantial domed reception area or grand gallery that stretched out and splitting into two adjacent corridors.

"This is just the same as those salt mines in Sardinia, where for some deranged reason the local inhabitants carved and designed the insides of the many caves like a bloody church," remarked Madelyn, as she straightened her left shoe back on her foot.

"That's because the people had to pray in secret. If they were caught praying above ground they would have been simply slaughtered by the ruling factions, so they built their churches underground. It's not unusual, we did the same in middle Briton throughout the dark days of history," remarked Erica, pointing the torch toward a panel that reflected a large Templar seal embossed into the soft salty sandstone. Madelyn just stared on trying to conjure up an image of a hundred or so people ascending into the many caverns in order just to pray.

She then traced the outer edge of the great Templar seal with her hand and found that it was very smooth to the touch, but, then noticed that the cross within the writing scrollwork sat quite proud of the actual embossed lettering and slowly eased it clock ways with her thumb, it moved ever so slightly then she stopped.

"Erica come here quick take a quick look at this the cross thingy, it moves, look you can rotate the writing within the seal."

Madelyn eased the cross to the left and rotated the inner circle a full 360 degrees then a distinct 'klunk' was heard from somewhere deep within the chamber.

"Careful, I don't like this kinda shit, it gives me the bloody creeps."

A few moments later and the great seal had been automatically and very mysteriously retracted back into the wall recess; obviously by the sound of the stone on stone and vibrations of what felt like a small earth tremor, and what appeared to sound like wooden blocks and tackle being moved around under a really heavy weight load.

A series of mechanisms, as the seal was being manipulated by a distant set of pulleys and winches, then within a few short moments a single, solid stone doorway, had appeared in the facia not twenty foot or so off to their immediate left.

"Well done girl," remarked Madelyn, as she stood closer to Erica then began shining her torch deep into the darkened chamber. The two ladies then took some time and quizzed the inner chamber and spied the adjacent annex: an antechamber that sat almost forty feet away into the rear of the vault.

"Don't like the look of that much, do you?" Erica said, softly.

Scattered across the floor were at least one hundred small chests and coffers, and a few substantial travelling cases which were stacked up to the left of the doorway. Erica was first to cough sneeze then speak again as she followed the light of the Maglite torch around the room.

"The floor seems to have lots of little bags spread everywhere, look, there and over there. Hang on, follow me. I think I can see a route through," remarked Erica, taking the lead and stepping forward heading towards the stack of wooden crates that appeared to have been hastily stored in the far corner to the left of the vault.

After a few minutes, their eyes had slowly but surely had become accustomed to the dimmed light and another glimmer of feint natural light had penetrated the chamber a few feet inwards.

From their stand point, the light appeared to be coming through a series of perforated panels high above them which had been somehow housed into the roof structure. Around them, the many shadows played tricks on their eyes as they slowly traversed the underground chambers.

"Look at this place it's like a bloody rabbit warren, or that shopping centre in the middle of Aberdeen or one of those bloomin, mythical labyrinth things. You know, this is probably twice as bad as—in fact, it's worse than hell's bloody half acre," she spouted, momentarily spitting a piece of cobweb from her bottom lip whilst trying to negotiate a path through the vault.

"God, you can say that again," replied Madelyn, as she stooped down and picked up something from the floor.

"What have you found there, lady?" asked Erica.

Madelyn took a bit of time, then answered. "Not sure, I think it's a key."

The two ladies quizzed the key then watched in almost desperation as the entrance door began closing automatically and very quickly, momentarily entrapping them both within the confides of the now darkened potential tomb. They knew they were too far away to escape the stoned vault and froze in their steps and gazed at each other.

"Don't worry! Maddy, these Knights were clever people they would not simply permit themselves to be locked within their own tombs, they would not build a vault that was capable of entrapment, trust me I have seen enough films on engineering to know better, but it may take some time for us to find our way out," remarked Erica, placing the key in her jacket pocket.

She then pushed her hair to one side and removed a Galaxy chocolate bar from her clutch bag.

"You hungry?" she asked, offering a healthy, four squares of the endorphin releasing chemicals.

"Oh yes, cannot resist chocolate, and Galaxy too, and so soon after breakfast, I must have been nice in a previous life," she said, then ate two squares of the cocoa mixed bar.

"So how come you and Kemp are together anyway? I am quite surprised he asked me to tag along. He is bright enough to sort this one out himself," quizzed Erica, in an effort to find out more about the eligible bachelor and probably to test Madelyn's emotions towards him.

"Oh, we have worked together several times now. We have investigated a few odd circumstances. Did you not investigate that Hellfire Sword thing last year with him?"

Erica smiled. "Don't mention that bloody episode—that was a certifiable nightmare, and a period in my life where I do not want to dwell on. I was kidnapped and drugged by some deranged druid who had doped me up beyond belief, and was saying that I was being taken to the stars in his starship. And did Kemp tell you we nearly got murdered, and I got . . ."

She then kicked up some dust and started to trace the wall recesses searching for a lock or a mechanism that could trip the door. "Nope not talking about it, blew me completely off the planet for ages, anyway what are we going to do now? Need to find an 'out' as they say."

"Do you know much about the history of The Knights' Templar?" asked Madelyn, as she flicked her long hair backwards then massaged the nape of her neck.

Erica interjected. "I have done a bit of study since our good Mr Hastings dragged me into a world of which I had no idea even actually existed. I have learned that as a biblical tutor you don't always believe what you read and that's a fact. But having said that, I had no idea you had come into the Order either, no that was all of a sudden wasn't it? It was just a week ago that I was approached for my scholastic background."

Madelyn dropped her head momentarily. "The very same thing happened to me, and that was about a week ago too. I think we have been manipulated. I wonder if it is to help Kemp find the original 'Templari Thesaurus' inventory? It could be that the Temple maybe have really lost the document, and are desperate to secure it before those Krouts or Arabs actually get their hands on it."

Erica was nodding and agreeing. "Sounds perfectly rational to me."

Madelyn continued discussing what she knew about the order and a bit of general overview of Scottish history. "Did you know that in the early reformation days of Scotland according to several Scottish historical documents the Knights Templar were amongst the most famous people in history? People like James of Claverhouse or Bonnie Dundee Grand Prior of Scotland murdered at Killiecrankie.

Bonnie Prince Charlie and Victor Hugo and Leonardo Di Vinci, amongst others, turn up somewhere in the historical records. The succession Order, written by the Knights, clearly depicted Bonnie Dundee's successor as 'The Earl of Mar' whose family, incidentally, still runs a private army that supports the Order today. That dashing Colonel Marquis being one of them, he is a bit of alright, don't you think?"

Madelyn thought for a few moments and contemplated the dashing Colonel's upper class, pompous attitude and his charming good looks against Hasting's sense of humour, physique and general attitude and then she smiled. "I don't know. I really like Kemp's playful, boyish smile. He tends to get all serious then goes to pieces once he has solved a particular problem.

I like the way he attacks problems head on, no messing he just gets the damn job done, then thanks the world for their help—he is sort of caring that way. No, I honestly think Kemp is more manly and sensitive at times than Captain Chaos. And he smells so nice too; he uses that Armani cool water, really fresh." Madelyn stopped herself swooning in case Erica thought there was a more intimate relationship developing between them and walked slowly toward the far recess in the void.

"Of course, the Colonel could invite you to all those stuffy higher class balls and functions they attend—all trussed up like chickens in their mess dresses and ball gowns—all too fancy for me I am afraid. I prefer a man in the kilt."

They both smiled and almost burst into a giggled frenzy in girly fashion as Erica continued the story.

"Anyway, Scottish history is a fascinating subject. Did you know that during this succession a new movement was afoot within what is now Great Britain and unionism was on the lips of all concerned leaders? This was a time when Scotland and England were sorting their alliance stuff out. The older, documented history of 'union' between Scotland and England, and not forgetting Wales, is known as 'The Treaty of Union' which sets out the future game plan for the political union of the countries in question and took effect on 1st May, 1707.

The 'nitty gritty' details of which were agreed 22nd July 1706, and passed between the governing bodies, the parliaments of Scotland and England in order to ratify the process of treaty. As these earlier warring nations started an integration process, the Knights' Templar had placed themselves very strategically behind the ascending royal families of both countries whilst forging a complicated internal union of their own.

Hugues De Payen had written several semi-rules or regulations to compliment how the Order was to function and described a true Knight as such: 'A Templar Knight is truly brave and fearless. He is secure, both mentally and physically and balanced on all sides. His 'soul' is protected by his armour of faith, and his physical form by the chain and armour of steel.

This will provide him the competence and confidence to support the many Kings and Queens that are to employ our services. Each Knight is therefore doubly armed and need fear neither man or demons whilst performing his defensive and protective duties."

Madelyn and Erica discussed the further aspects of being females within the order but somehow felt that they were forming a new side of the 21st century development of Christendom to meet the needs of the modern world.

The succession of Dames within the order was an amazing step for The Knights' Templar to take and each rank had the same role as the male. A role that was designed originally for a hired swordsman and killer.

Erica pondered for a moment on their current endeavour and smiled. "Goodness, Maddy, we are actually caught up in modern day history, if you think about it."

Ironically, they were now both caught up in more of an adventure that would rival a good James Bond movie script, than an actual audit, and of which, incidentally, neither of the girls actually wanted to be Bond girls anyway. Purely because Ian Fleming had a strange view of the woman's role in his books and kept killing them off willy nilly. 'And that was not a good thing,' thought Maddy, shining the torch toward an opening in the far wall.

After a brief period in the bone yard, Hastings wandered through most of the cemetery searching for the girls and assumed that they had entered the chapel to view the gold and internal trappings of the wee church.

It was not until he realised that the door had been tied with a single plastic tie wrap that something was definitely not right. Ripping the tie wrap with his fingers he hurriedly entered the building and found it very quiet and serene, apart from the gaping hole in the back of the altar wall everything was in good shape.

"Oh ladies—what are you two up to now? Damn women! Just cannot leave them alone for five minutes—they only had to wait a few moments."

He stepped through the bolt hole and found his pen-lite torch and switched it on. He then wandered the inner vaults within the church walls. It was after about nine minutes or so before he could hear the distant voices of women talking in the background. He stopped, then listened intently as the voices seemed to resonate through the adjacent wall and were becoming louder.

He continued to walk slowly through the tunnel heading for what appeared to be larger chamber at the end of the stone hallway, just where the path branched in three directions. Instinctively he chose the middle path and walked stealthily through the cavern which began to turn left.

Once he reached a point where all the arches widened, he spotted a single chest sitting on a nearby stone ledge. Scattered around the bottom of the box was a series of footprints and paper cuttings which appeared to have been dropped in the sand. Over to his right, he spied another heavy duty casket.

It appeared to Hastings to be an older style ammunition box which was two foot wide and four foot in length. Hastings wiped some sand off the top of the box and read the writing. It had been clearly labelled with the markings of the SS Swastika and an odd 'Templar Kross' based on the Teutonic Order of the ancient world.

The markings on each case was complimented by a neatly stamped stencil that ran along the external leading edge of the box and displayed the word 'Geheim' in bold red lettering

The skull or Totenkopf insignia was clearly visible and had been stamped into the actual moulding of the trunk.

He reverently opened the lid to the kiste and to his surprise found a few pages of parchment paper and a book on naval warfare. The items were leaning upright and to one side of the box. On further inspection, he found a piece of flattened rose wood which caught his immediate attention. He picked it up and viewed its surface.

From his vast knowledge of symbology and folklore, he instantly recognised the fabled markings of the 'DM code' which had been etched into the soft wood. He was slightly taken by surprise as he had decided years ago that the tale of the Shugborough code and any real ties to the Anson family and the Order was a complete hoax.

He whispered to himself the letters: "D—OUOSVAVV—M the shepherd's monument, NOSTRADAMUS refers to ancient cave—chambers of Roslin. What was it that Pouissin intimated toward: 'et in arcadia ego' roughly translated—I too am in Arcadia. Or the anagram: I keep God's secrets . . . nope cannot get my head around that one."

Hastings was unconvinced, but could not understand how this code came to be in this particular church in the middle of Switzerland, let alone be etched to a piece of rosewood. He rubbed his chin and thought about Poussini and recalled the letter he had penned.

The letter itself explaining the code somewhere in the year 1635, and alluded to the position of the fingers of the people in the picture, and perhaps more importantly the missing letters and whatever outcomes could be deduced.

He then thought about the many depositories that the Order would have quite happily used to hide their riches, especially in haste if they were being pursued by the French King's troops. The most famous being the Chateau Le Rennes.

Sauniere's church actually contains a daemon guardian in its confines. It consists of a single statue of 'Asmodeus' and is responsible for the optical illusion of the blue apples, where it is said, at noon, the light beams through the stained glass windows casting the images of blue apples.

Sauniere was clearly not the brains behind the madcap idea of exploiting money from the masses, it was more of a scam by the PoS—The Priory of Sion, who were very active and Father Henri Boudet was perhaps the brains behind the venture as a PoS Activist.

The Parish priest of Rennes Les Baines was indeed deemed a crank antiquarian who argued that English was the predominant language of the world, stemming from ancient Celts. Hastings did not dismiss his intellectual use of symbology and ciphers and had used his methods several times in cracking otherwise un-crackable codes.

Other documents Hastings had acquired regarding the PoS suggested that after his death in 1918, that artist, poet and film maker Jean Cocteau became the incumbent Grand Master of the Priory and partnered two rather interesting artists by the name of Picasso for art and Erik Satie for music.

Pablo Picasso for an extended period of time denoted his artistic talents toward esoteric and obscure mythological themes, and was said to have been influenced by Cocteau himself. Erik Satie was influenced to mix and match and improvised some of Claude Debussy's work and re-arranged his music the 'Le six' as an example. The inextricable link to the PoS Grand Masters was indeed Erik Satie.

His mind darted back to a recent paper on the castle at Gisors, in France. Another angle was that Roget Lenoir, the then caretaker, must have had access to at least one of the 'Templari Thesaurus' codex documents or had acquired a copy of an ancient map of where the temple laid its riches to rest.

Perhaps the map that the Germans or the not so Teutonic Order had in their possession when the Colonel of the secret Army intercepted them, he then remembered his yellow Nokia mobile which the so called Knights had passed on to him. He found the phone and dialled the only number in its address list.

A few moments later a voice answered. "Hello, guten tag. Can I help you?"

Just then the church bells pealed in the back ground. He stared at his watch then thought that it must have been about nine of clock. Hastings waited until the bells had stopped, then spoke into the phone. "This is Hastings, I was wondering if your map thingy has the details of the Fren . . ." He then broke off his conversation as the bells pealed again, having worked out that the phone line at the other end of the line became much clearer as the bells in the background had stopped ringing exactly at the same time as the ones in the church yard had. Even the peal tone was the same and had chimed at the same time, just as he was talking to the Germans. He closed the mobile down.

"Shit, if those are the same bells, then those buggers are topside waiting on us."

He then dialled Erica's mobile number: no answer. He then dialled Madelyn's phone. There was still no answer and he began to think the worst case scenario and panicked slightly as he started to dash towards wherever the tunnel ended.

As he scurried through the tunnels, he was thinking that the map from Gisors was rumoured to reflect the 'crypt' under Roslin chapel or Solomon's temple itself, or another location somewhere in Europe.

It was definitely a place where a group of Knights had been interred along with great riches, and also a very long time ago, and then the tomb was simply but effectively filled with tons upon tons of sand. Could that be the imaginative and protective response by the 4th Earl of Roslin to keep ritual in balance?

Hasting had visited Gisors several years back and had researched the older graffiti that had been etched into the walled surfaces of the Gisors walled masonry, to the effect that even Victor Hugo himself had visited the castle to endorse and approve any research, and to support what may have been a sanctioned excavation by the holy Order.

However, his visit was double bubble and endorsed by his etching of his name 'twice' on the walled surfaces, not a normal act of moronic vandalism for a visitor to undertake, especially to an otherwise insignificant building, but why sign his name twice, unless he visited twice? Hastings sniffed then coughed and closed his mobile.

Rumours recorded that perhaps 19 x stone Sarcophagi and several chests of money were discovered in the Gisor's castle, but the Order may have had relocated them very quickly leaving an empty chamber for Lenior to explain to the Ministry having declared an incredible find of great wealth.

That was the one and only time in history that the Temple could have nearly lost its holdings. It would have taken a swift, concerted military effort to clear the vault of the many items, again removed in the wee small hours of the French morning dew, and conducted very quickly under a blanket of utmost silence and secrecy.

If popular rumour was to be acted upon then thousands upon thousands of treasure-seekers will descend on Gisors and Nova Scotia in the near future, or to be more precise Oak island in Nova Scotia in particular which is a location used as a back drop to just more than a series of swashbuckling sagas in search of Templar riches.

Many scholars have been trapped in their engineering capabilities having deciphered several codes where it was clear that the elaborate construction of the money pit was certainly designed to hide a great secret and constructed by the greatest minds on the planet who possessed a very potent and intellectual capacity of the ancient Order.

The Arcadian Shepherd's mystery is pretty much in the open and even Hastings had considered investing in the project several years back. The outcome would be information only.

And consisted of: a location near the east coast within a French colony, where some artefacts belonging to St John's inherited worldly goods . . . at L'Acadia or Philadelphia—and with the blessings of the MICMAC Indians in and around, 1795—a place to start a new crusade where the infamous money pit is located.

And he thought it was all too complicated or simply pie in the eternal sky. His mind was running amok and a mess of information and statistics were being hurled around his brain box and was clearly inhibiting his train of rationale thought.

Hastings walked on and eventually reached the inner vaults and his mind had gone totally blank; he was annoyed and pissed off at the same time. He felt he was being led on a wild goose chase and although the Temple picked up the bill for his efforts, his internal thinking and logical mind—map had begun filtering information.

His logical train of thought was in literal tatters, and he could just simply not think straight.

His only real secret being 'what he had just discovered at the grave site of St Bernard's pseudo grab-stein, in Andermatt', where his efforts to search his gut instinct and urges had paid off, and again his attention to simple detail was crucial, but again he knew that his choice of locations might have been manipulated by the Order.

He thought he had the upper hand. But still knew that his life was in danger as was Dr Toadie's, until he discovered the inventory parchment and was murdered as a result. Hastings had to act swiftly and remain one step ahead of the two Teutonic maniacs who wanted nothing but money and to see him dead.

He stopped walking as he heard the feint noise of tapping against the nearby wall. He shouted and heard the distinctive tones of Erica's slightly high pitched, girly voice echoing somewhere not too far away. He shouted out. "Erica, its Kemp, where are you guys?"

Erica, on hearing his voice, skipped hastily to the vault's entrance recess and stopped then shouted back. "The Great Seal, spin the Great Seal's inner collar . . . turn it clockwise, three and a quarter turns, no more than that. It should be enough!" she yelled, louder than her normal calm pitched tone.

In no time at all, Hastings had found the seal and placed a hand on the inner bezel and began to spin the stone ring anti-clockwise. He muttered to himself as he quizzed his watch to check the time, then paid attention to the great seal as he slowly executed the unlock sequence.

"Three, point, one, four, five . . . that should do it," he said quietly, and watched the walls for any movements as the distant 'klunks' of the heavy, archaic steel mechanism caught his earshot. Within a few moments, the vault door was opened and he was being groped and cuddled by the two nicest women on the planet: the two females that he actually liked being around.

"Ladies, ladies please, great to see you alive, but what in God's name are you two doing down here?"

After a careful explanation from Erica, the trio took stock of their environment and predicament. They had agreed that the German visitors were indeed very hostile and that they were somewhere still near to the church, and must have followed them to Switzerland from Scotland.

As they found their way back out of the vault and back into the grave yard, Hastings slowly took time to give the surrounding area another quick once over before he exited the doorway.

All appeared to be quiet until they reached the inner village of Andermatt and were in the process of arranging a trip to see the Devil's bridge when Dr Vine recognised one of the German activists in the hotel lobby.

Luckily for her, he had not seen her loitering in the foyer and she had literally dived into the toilets out of sight in a ditch attempt not to be recognised or caught in the hotel Krone.

Meanwhile, Hastings was busy saying hello to hotel owners Rolf and Sally Solinger in the main entrance hallway, they had actually managed the hotel back in the early seventies and still personally welcomed guests to their beautiful Krone hotel, and they remembered Hastings as a younger and somewhat fitter man.

Hastings was awash with emotions and had found himself walking the out houses and ski storage room that had been built with its own nuclear bunker and was stocked with enough food stuffs that were stashed to feed an army of fat soldiers for years to come—of course that was if they had to live underground for months on end.

CHAPTER EIGHTEEN

Madelyn's Research

B ack in the hotel room, Madelyn searched her clutch bag and eventually found what she was looking for as she raked amongst lipsticks, a torch, her iPod and a range of cosmetics that would normally keep Mary Quant unblemished for many years to come, then located the folded up document.

Erica, meanwhile, had jumped into the shower and was busy pampering herself after the odd day's events. Madelyn pulled out the brochure which depicted a series of photographs and articles regarding the lost spoils of war and of which was mainly centred around Toplitze and the Nazi involvement.

She browsed a few articles on the subject then drew circles around what she thought could be helpful as a contribution as part of Hastings's work. She compiled a portfolio for some background information and further understanding if it was required.

Hastings had a notion about great wealth being retrieved from various sources and locations and knew that not all details were a fantasy and considerable efforts were made to corroborate his ideas, as to how the Order cared for its multifaceted, inventory, and he knew the process of how to procure and record it all, and was simply quite overwhelming in its concept.

By Erica's reckoning, this one haul at Toplitz could make up for approximately sixteen per cent of the Order's coffers. She read an article whereupon an

American fighter plane was targeted and shot down and was rumoured to be carrying Hitler's final mail delivery of booty.

The Junker 88 is recorded as being destroyed on 5th May 1945, and is still said to be located in a glacier high up in the Alps. She grabbed her pen then drew a big circle around the article then crossed it out, dismissing it as a location that was unlikely to be visited by the order.

The cargo was said to be worth 500,000,000 gold francs and platinum ingots somewhere near Aussess 37 miles from Salzburg, but too complicated to locate. She searched three other documents and articles and discovered that two years later, in the January of 1932, eleven of the previous members of the Trinity of the Tower came together to form the 'L'Ordre Souverain et Militaire du Temple de Jerusalem.' Or, alternatively the 'Sovereign Military Order of the Temple of Jerusalem' and, to which they invited those members who had remained with their parent Order du Temple, including the Grand Priories of Portugal, Italy and Switzerland.

In March 1935, the new Order had appeared to have been re-established and slowly began to flourish under the Regent Theodore Covias followed by Emile Isaac Vandenberg, who became Regent also in that year, and not long after which, he was elected Grand Master by the October.

It was unfortunate for him that World War II interrupted his tenure, and there were great concerns as the Order knew that Hitler and his high ranking Nazis were nuts on the macabre, esoteric and damn right strange aspects of society and displayed an unhealthy relationship toward the Occult.

The Nazi regime expended huge amounts of resource and energy in various attempts to track down knowledge and any items of significant power, and had very early on in their occupation targeted the Order.

As a result of this unwanted attention, the Order formulated a plan to send its worth to the Grand Prior in Portugal, to Antonio Campello Pinto de Sousa Fontes, whereupon, a decree was executed by GM E.I. Vandenberg December 1942 to ensure its safe transit.

It was during an untimely car accident, near Brussels, that Vandenberg was killed and succession had automatically been passed on with little or no information afforded to the receiver. Antonio Fontes remained Regent as incumbent GM until his own death in February 1960, and was succeeded by his 'alter ego'—his son, Fernando.

Madelyn then picked out a picture that was stuck in the file and gazed upon the photograph of the older Fernando, and thought to herself that he was a good looking man for his years. She read the final portion of the document and made a frenzy of notes in her little red book:

> *Antonio Fontes remained as Regent with the prerogatives of Grand Master until his death in February of 1960 when he was succeeded by his son Fernando, the current Grand Master, who received official endorsements from the senior officers of the Order in 1960.*

She then pulled out two further documents and placed them on the table.

ORDRE SOUVERAIN ET MILITAIRE DU TEMPLE DE JÉRUSALEM

GRANDE MAITRISE
GRAND PRIEURÉ DE PORTUGAL

Nós, abaixo assinados, Grandes Priores da Ordem Soberana e Militar do Templo de Jerusalem (ORDO SUPREMUS MILITARIS TEMPLI HIEROSOLYMITANI) e visto a fotogravura da acta-sucessoria do nosso Regente D. Antonio Campello, reconhecemos como sucessor e nosso legitimo Regente, D.Fernando Campello Pinto Pereira de Souza Fontes, assim designado e prometemos a nossa lealdade e colaboração para que o nome da Ordem possa ser respeitado e ocupe na Sociedade o seu justo lugar cultural, historico e cavalheiresco. Feito em duplicado, bastando a assinatura de num.

As she quizzed the documents, what caught her eye was the 'Toplitz article'. For some reason Hastings had a bee in his bonnet and was convinced in his mind that the Knights had indeed brought a consignment of this haul to Scotland, and he himself owned several silver 1945 Reichsbank coins which he thought may have been part of the haul.

Hastings took great pride in showing Madelyn his own collections of coins and paperwork during her last visit to his home, perhaps maybe, in an attempt to gain her attentions, but was very much overshadowed by the recent exposure to the new batch of solid gold coins passed on by the man in the doorway at the Fisher King's building. And it was bugging them both as to why the Fisher Kings held the coins in the first place.

Madelyn pulled out several newspaper cuttings from an older envelope and read the contents with greater interest. One article had been fully ringed using a black pen with the words 'Farcical' written off to one side. It read:

In July of the year 1959, an expedition of German technicians were working with high tech, ultrasound equipment of varying descriptions including modular depth finders and CCTV which pinpointed 16 x cases in Lake Toplitz, Austria.

Once the cases were brought to surface, the estimated haul was approximately 8,500,00 pounds of 'forged' British bank notes, and was possibly intercepted by the underground movements either French or Italians. Then dumped back into the deep waters on the authority provided by the joint services of British and American Commanders, in order to prevent saturation of the British economy throughout the warring period.

What still remains a conundrum is the whereabouts of the other treasures that accompanied this consignment, some of which included a cache of billions in gold, gems and art work, and it could of course still be a possibility that a good portion of the wealth could still be at the bottom of the lake pending discovery, and lay deep within the Styrian Alps.

The question that hangs on the lips of the modern day treasure seeking community is: 'Was Hitler's treasure of the Third Reich dumped into Lake Toplitz near the Devil's Trashcan in the Syrian Alps or not? Not only the cache of billions in gold, gems and other valuables, but additionally, secret war records, more importantly the 'Kriegs papierwerk' of the Nazi party. All of which were apparently encased in waterproof cases. Again a question to ask is: Why water proof cases?'

Madelyn cut her research short, thinking that one treasure map was enough, let alone fifteen of them and closed the informative brochures and placed them back in her bag along with her stack of newspaper cuttings and her Eves St Laurent and Coco Chanel collection of bottles.

She located her iPad and web searched some more interesting articles, soon to discover that the 'SS' were rife in disposing of their assets and their co-conspirators, especially towards what was becoming the end of the great war, whilst harbouring every notion of recouping their losses in the years that would follow the 'Blitzkreig'.

In world terms, she found that the British Army was actually in retreat from the Nazi regime and had just finished invading Greece, where Churchill had almost 15 divisions of deployed troops and serious aggressive hardware along with 900 aircraft in support, this manoeuvre was being engineered just as the German war machine invaded the mountains of Thessalonika.

It was recorded that during this forward thrust, a single truck carrying three grey boxes and two larger crates which retained the British Army's payroll and a large quantity of sovereigns and bullion had been compromised and was a consignment which had been entrusted into Greek hands in order to ship the booty abroad.

It was during an impromptu attack that the custodians were forced to place the payroll and the riches into a cave and subsequently sealed the contents up. By orchestrating a series of explosions using hand grenades to bring down tons upon tons of rocks and seal the stone void completely, the location was said to be near to mount Siniatsikon near Korani.

Madelyn took a deep breath and continued in her web search to reveal that the treasure was valued at over $2,500,000 and still remains buried today. Of course, she was now a little wiser, having found several gold sovereigns and a Wehrmacht military ausweiss along with a gravestone receipt. And copious amounts of documents belonging to a British Gunner called Anthony Gerrard, who had been attached to the Intelligence Corps in 1943; could this be the dead man from the Fisher Kings? She recalled Hastings had removed his wallet.

She found a few more other snippets and jotted down her findings, as any good researcher would. Not only was she amused by the sheer volume of gold and riches that was being moved around Europe but, as to why every consignment appeared to have been intercepted during any transit operations. It was clear that The Knights' Global Templar Order were perhaps working fervently in the backdrop to disrupt any transit of high dollar inventory and to procure and secure the wealth of a nation with or without compromise.

She also noted that several submarines had traversed the Pacific Coast during a concise period in war time, and were rumoured that one vessel in particular contained several paintings by the artist Van Dyke and were valued at a colossal 500,000,000 francs and may well be still secreted on one of the islands of the Marquis as Archipelago, somewhere in the Pacific ocean.

The vessel could have been the registered U-Boat U-435 which sank offshore during a deliberate bombing raid. Again a hit that was orchestrated by the allied forces under an obscure and very controversial German telegram which held some sensitive and exacting details, which apparently fell into the wrong hands, or the right hands depending on which side of the war effort one sits within.

CHAPTER NINETEEN

The Max Heiliger Account

T he Colonel, from the Atholl Mar's secret army, contacted Hastings and had furnished him the location of where the two Germans had taken up local residence, apparently the accommodation had been rented for over four months and appeared to be uninhabited up until recently.

The note supplied by Colonel Marquis had the address of the apartment and the name written on the doorplate. It read: 'Heiliger.

Hastings slowly made his way up through the building's dark stairwell to the top floor then carefully listened before he 'jemmied' the door open to Flat number 16, and had managed to unlatch the lock with his trusty Swiss army knife.

He glanced at the name plate again. It said: 'Max Heiliger'. He smiled a smirk of contempt.

Entering the flat, he carefully made his way into the living room. Having listened for any sign of inhabitants, he decided the coast was clear and moved stealthily through the apartment, but was momentarily stunned at what he saw laid out before him.

Sitting on the central coffee table was a set of medieval ledgers all written in the German language; to compliment this library of books were some war time photographs.

They were obviously older documents and they had been bound together with a red ribbon which had been crossed wrapped around the middle of each individual book.

Lying to the left of the ledgers were several account documents that appeared to be facsimile copies of statements from the Swiss National Bank. Hastings took several photographs using his mobile telephone and sent them on to Madelyn for a quick analysis and feedback.

After a few minutes Madelyn had called him back.

"Hey, Kemp, can you hear me? Right, got some details here for you. All those pictures you sent me, they are actual documents that allude to the Max Heiliger account. And here is the scary bit: the 'M' accounts, or the actual Max Heiliger accounts, were the 'SS' secret bank accounts that were used during world war II to finance the Blitzkreig.

These German treasure seekers are shooting away off their mark if they think the Knights' Templar have taken stock of this horde of gold in the UK, because along with those documents there are also the 'J' accounts or Judengold (Jew's Gold), and, Kemp, that is real time blood money or blut gold, it will only bring heartache and misery to anyone involved with this booty.

The bank accounts consisted of the deposits removed from the 'Jews' during the Blitz. It was an account for holding all the personal jewellery, and precious gems from dead prisoners and their belongings stolen by those 'SS' bastards from Auschwitz, Dachau or Belsen and other concentration camps. This was when the Wehrmacht ethnically cleansed their way into the history books."

Madelyn stopped talking and sniffed at the air. Hastings thought her voice had become slightly stressed and a bit more emotional as she explained her findings.

"You be careful there, Kemp. Anyway, the other ledgers are disposition documents—that's a ledger, Kemp, or an agreement with the Swiss national banking system. The 'M' lettering also relates to the Melmer or Max Heiliger accounts, and as I said, stinks of 'SS' management.

It also looks like Goering signed the majority of these documents himself." She paused again, then continued updating Hastings as to what he was looking at in the pictures of the flat of the German treasure seekers. "Do you think these idiots actually think the Order has this gold sitting in their churches?" She then paused and waited for Hastings to respond.

Hastings remained quiet and was thinking about where the connection lies. Why would they think the Order here in Scotland would have this particular horde of war bullion and coins? What could possibly trigger such a mad cap campaign?

Madelyn interjected. "Now, Kemp, there is one document letter that's states 'Monetary Gold'. Can you find it and read out again? I need to hear or see the middle paragraphs 16 to 20 starts with the words 'indenture' then followed by some figures . . . ."

Hastings located the document and read out a few short paragraphs, then stopped reciting his findings.

Madelyn quickly interjected again.

"Kemp, these documents are copies of some of the paperwork that was presented at the Nuremberg War Trials. Someone very high up in the legal system provided our visitors with access to this documentation, because it is not easy for just anyone to get access to these archives, let alone obtain copies of them.

We are dealing with an orchestrated effort by some higher echelons here. Kemp, there is something else I think you should know, the 'Gold Pool', which was a huge chunk of cash, which consisted of nearly 5.5 tons of mixed gold bars and coins, that was used to compensate, where practical, the victims of the war, but also included the gold deposits from Germany's domestic bank accounts.

And not just the Nazi gold deposits in Switzerland, but all the gold bullion and coins found under Nazi Germany's control. I think this is where our Teutonic friends must have got their wires crossed. It would not surprise me if they think that this gold still physically exists. I mean Reichsbank coins and gold, platinum and silver bullion bars in their original form and simply lying around in vaults and coffers dotted over Europe is quite absurd, let alone to be stored here in Scotland.

My guess is that they probably think that although there was many agencies tasked to dispense the gold back to the qualifying recipients post war Germany, and, they, our visitors somehow might think that the Order was an agency working under that charity banner, albeit, each charity was given over 6 million dollars to distribute accordingly. I am not sure if the Templars were part of these groups."

As Madelyn chatted away, Hastings was still scouting the small living space for any other signs or indicators that could help him determine what was actually going on. He spied another document sitting under the remnants of a McDonald's happy meal on the table. He picked up the file and read its contents out loudly, the paper was a report named:

Note: on Gold Operations involving the bank for international settlements & The German Reichsbank—dated: 1939-1945.

He thanked Madelyn for her assistance and then flicked his phone shut.

He then read to page 12 of the document before being alerted by the arrival of a car in the car park below. He gazed out of the window and spied the two Germans walking towards the building, and they were accompanied by a shapely, blonde female.

"Typical, that makes sense BMW to Mercedes, Germans so bloody predictable, but who is this girl?"

He then grabbed the 'Note: document' and left the confines of the flat, ensuring to lock the door on his way out.

As he exited the rear entrance of the building, his phone vibrated as it received an incoming message. He flicked the Nokia open and read the message.

CHAPTER TWENTY

'Trap'

Erica Vine, awoke in a fit of fear; she had been roused out of her sleep very abruptly just as the sticky tape was applied across her mouth and her hands were momentarily tie wrapped together. She attempted to struggle but it was futile, she was trussed up like an oven bound turkey and very distressed.

The two assailants were slick and clean and had immobilised her within forty seconds after entering her flat. They had meticulously carried out their research and executed their well-rehearsed task just before 5 am.

There was no real aggression on the part of her captors; they just left a cold atmosphere that had triggered her very worst innermost fears. She stared on as the two masked men, searched the room opening drawers and cupboard spaces, her eyes were flirting from the doorway to the window, then at the two men, she observed that they were relatively muscled clad men, their attire was plain black jacket and slacks, nothing sinister apart from the fact that they appeared cold and calibrated.

After a few short minutes, they soon left her flat with her car keys and her spare laptop in their possession. Her mind was racing, fearful of having either being raped or murdered, and she had no idea if they had gone on were going to return.

As the masked men left her flat, she realised that her legs had also been tie-wrapped to the bed posts. She was breathing very deeply and sweating profusely. After several minutes of wriggling to try and break free, she closed her eyes and wept.

Outside the building the two men were met by another single, white female.

"Did you get the keys and the computer?" she asked, aiming her line of questioning toward the taller of the two soldiers of fortune.

"Yep, she is hogtied—just as you asked."

"Have you touched her or harmed her in any way?"

The reply was clear and direct. "No, she has been left exactly as you explained. We even left the lights on in the living room, and pulled the phone cable. Of course, we swiped her car keys and her iPad, nothing more. She will be worried and a bit mentally disturbed for a while, but apart from that she is physically unharmed," explained the German, as he tossed the keys at the girl.

"Good job—well done. Now the pantomime begins. Do you have all your bits and bobs with you? I have checked the messages on her mobile phone: it appears she is to meet that journalist woman at eleven o'clock, tomorrow.

I do not know where the Church Street actually is in the village of Brechin, so, I suggest you get there pretty early, and once you find the street, text us we will be nearby at the Cathedral.

So, once you send that journalist paper woman a text of where you are and when to meet, then when you arrive, we will ensure that Mr Hastings is also alerted. We need about an hour or so to give him time to get there."

The lady gazed at her sister's mobile phone and smiled.

"Just as we planned. I will see you back at the apartment, now go pack all the ledgers and clear up all our crap. I will drop by later this evening and pick the documents up; once we get that inventory we are on 'easy street'."

CHAPTER TWENTY ONE

John Erskine (1ˢᵗ Earl of Mar)
c.1510-1572

Hastings retrieved his audit report from the desk drawer and sat down. He skimmed over what he had written and corrected a few typing errors he had made. He found it almost negligible not to mention some of the keepers and their squires or indeed the unsung heroes and people who had silently supported the Order up into modern day, and paused for thought before continuing in his cryptic ramblings.

He then flicked over his notes a few times more and stopped on a page that was written in red ink: He then typed a few notes:

Regent of Scotland and keeper of Edinburgh and Stirling Castles, Mr John Erskine, a somewhat powerful man in the circles of political intrigue and deceit. A man who had been courted and groomed by both sides of the 'Union Coin' as the struggle between Mary of Lorraine and her protestant nobles ensued.

Erskine was created Earl of Mar by Her Majesty 'Mary Queen of Scots' in the year 1565, and was instrumental in her abdication only two years later. For whatever reasons, Mar chose to oppose Mary but history tells us that his pragmatism paved his way and he was given custody of the 'young James VI, and became Regent after the death of the Earl of Lennox.

Mar's family haunt the glens and hillsides of the Braemar that we observe today and we can rest assured that those ancient alliances and trusts will bond the Kinsmen and Clans well into the 22nd century, especially now that Scotland endures a bumpy, political rollercoaster ride into devolution.

An act that Mar perhaps would have liked to have witnessed after the efforts of the Clans in early 1320 to become an independent country.

Hastings captured a few more notes then picked the key points in the Orders existence and cogitated on the absolution attempt on the Order in the year 1307.

He then wrote his summary notation:

Final summary.

It would be prudent to note that since the revelation of the 'Chinon Parchments' in the late 1940's, the Chinon Revelation being a document which exposed a series of ancient dossiers exonerating the Order fully from all the trumped up charges served upon the Order.

However, due to a range of charges including ludicrous accounts of 'heresy to blasphemy' which were executed in a desperate futile attempt to discredit the Order as far as possible. The result being the trials primarily used as an excuse to strip and relieve the Order of their vast wealth.

Sadly, the Chinon parchment itself was mis-filed and came to light to too late in the grander scheme of things to assist and re-install the Order back into society at that time which meant the inventories may have sailed with the Templar Fleet at that time.

This meant that the early inventories of the many, many vaults and coffers were not readily available for view or accountancy, which have been lost or destroyed, having been shipped across the face of Christendom and lost in time.

For Scotland, I have viewed 123 x inventories, including Edinburgh and Stirling Castles, Falkland, Scone palaces and 12 x churches in Angus.

It was somewhat difficult to trace the actual custodians of The Knights' Templar—Ecosse consignments, however, I have managed to trace—146 x additional ledgers in the French Royal palace and have requested a viewing for later in the year 2012 or later.

However, having had access to the French dossiers of Champagne, I have found one inventory claiming to have recovered 123,000 French Francs from the Order, and had been placed as recently as the year 1993 in the Order's Swiss account as part of a reconciliation of funds campaign.

Therefore, if the Order was not so disrupted by many historical events, then it would have been a mundane task to simply account for the wealth of the Order by the copious amount of ledgers that The Knights' Templar have maintained.

I have reviewed 270 x ledgers, dating 1812 to 2010, and find the financial worth of the Templar inventory for Scotland to be estimated at $XXXXXXXXXXXX—

- *See enclosed ledgers for financial statements.*

It would also be very apt to state that those many loyal Knights and Dames involved in the management of the Order's inventory today have also kept sensitive information strictly to themselves, which is extremely encouraging and they are protecting information that is otherwise managed with all best intentions in the world to preserve human history.

A process of maintaining the integrity and intrinsic value of such relics, owned and secured under a strict code of internal Templar ethics and practices.

I submit the outcomes of this comprehensive audit contained on the enclosed DVD—Digital Versatile Disk—and have taken the liberty to capture electronically—locations, people and relics and our many riches that adorn our dusty coffers.

Signed,
Kemp Hastings 'alter ego' GM. 2012.

Non Nobis Domine, Non Nobis, Sed Nomini Tuo Da Gloriam!

CHAPTER TWENTY-TWO

Qumran Essenes

Hastings sat in quiet contemplation. His visit to the cemetery in Switzerland had furnished him with a hidden knowledge so awesome and unbelievable that he chose not to share his findings with either Madelyn or Erica. He felt that if they had an inclination of what was interred in the small Andermatt village cemetery then this could endanger their lives even more so.

He removed his phone and viewed the pictures he had taken from the 1940's gravesite. There were several pictures of the epitaph and, of which, were clearly not 'run of the mill'. They did not represent an interred person; there were no indicators of the deceased's life, or their profession or any reference to their next of kin or loved ones left behind.

Just the simple engraving of the 'Green Man' with the words: Qumran Essenes clearly depicted on the hogsback headstone.

What Hastings found was more interesting was the very small, Arabic type writing that ran along the base of the stone. It was either ancient Hebrew or Aramaic and what appeared to be some examples of Greek lettering. He was somewhat confused.

Hastings was thinking 'copper plate scrolls'. He was thinking 'biblical treasures' and information that could undo the very belief system of Christendom. He knew that almost 900 scrolls had been discovered somewhere in the caves at 'Qumran' deep in the Judean desert during the years 1947 to 1956, and the actual location was reported to be near to 'En Gedi' a place where the Dead Sea Scrolls were said to have actually been discovered as part of a deliberate investigative expedition.

But the documents and trinkets he had removed from the Green Man were something that would make biblical scholars scramble for academic cover; each scrambling and reaching for an umbrella made of solid steel for protection—as the myriad of real facts upon facts rained down upon the so called informed community.

He had uncovered another type of potent scroll completely and this was a 'Temple Scroll'; a document of certifiable fact with specific references to the first part or opening chapters to a much more comprehensive archaic document.

Hastings could decipher what he thought was a 'covenant' overview: a pact between God and the lands of Israel, and more importantly exacting details on the dimensions on a physical Temple, measurements and design information that alluded to the Holy of Holies or sanctuary.

In his many travels, he had wandered several times through both Judea and Jordan and had ventured into Iraq and Israel in his global trekking; he was not wholly inspired with the latter, but he felt somehow cleansed as he traversed through God's biblical lands. He would often explain to friends that this was his biblical calling, and yet he was not an 'out and out' devout person, but he had walked the many paths of the Apostles.

He thought that any visit through Jordan and into the Holy Land would trigger one's belief system in to thinking how the terrain could be easily used to hide a lot more than simple parchments, especially as the surrounding rocky escarpments were virtually littered with caves and nooks.

But with so much biblical baggage and spurious add-ons being applied through the ages, the terrain on its own actually makes one take a deep breath as one traverses through the mountainous backdrop as did the ancient population of Christendom.

A virtual tunnel network within the rock faces and where, even today, new discoveries are coming to light; each new artefact offering many challenging issues driven by the words of the ancient clerics.

Arguments based on facts from the time of Christ, we could touch on the Nag Hammadi in its entirety as a counter argument towards any documents of interest, and Hastings felt it prudent to leave this book and research as another bone of contention completely.

The 'Essenes' or Zadokite Priests, to give them their modern day names, are however a people more intriguing. They were not only the clerics who wrote the Dead Sea Scrolls but also were pragmatic enough to procure the complete collection and hide the scrolls away from any prying eyes whilst protecting the sensitive accounts of biblical life up through the ages.

An Order of religious Monks whose sole duty was to ensure that when the modern world was mature and educated enough. Then they would decipher the information and disseminate it amongst the global, academic masses to set the global historical records straight.

Whereupon, these scrolls would be released to scholars and academics, who are even today struggling to make good sense of the volatile and explosive detail of early Christian life, detail that reflected 'a time snapshot' with irrefutable evidence in the form of a written record.

One could compare the diary of Samuel Pepys in comparison to the written word as he recorded the Great fire of London in 1666 in exacting detail, and of which, not many scholars argue against his written words.

Therefore, why should the academics and eminent boffins of today really doubt the word of the people who were around at the same time of many biblical characters and were prepared to 'die' for their proverbial beliefs and their omnipotent God?

Although, at this point in time, there are no actual documents in existence to prove that the Essenes actually wrote the Dead Sea Scrolls, and the question to pose is: "If they did not write them, then who did?"

Hastings went off on one his few mind boggling tangents and threw his thoughts into the quagmire of information that he was trying so desperately to separate in his mind's eye.

"Bloody arsehole scholars, if McDonald's produce a menu, then obviously McDonald's were instrumental in designing it and writing it. How anal can people get?"

He thought about the humble 'Essenes' who chose to live an impoverished life, then renounced their worldly belongings and promoted self-sufficiency. They even administered some vows of chastity. They were, in essence, an ancient sect—that The Knights' Templars of ancient days could aspire to become. The Essenes were a classic example of a society that embraced the ethos of 'sustainable development'.

He was convinced that the Essenes had secreted their great wealth in the mosque at Al Aqsa. They took time to carefully bury their biblical booty deep down within the rocky escarpment of Temple mount, and could have passed this location to the Templar's in exchange for protection.

And of which, the vast riches were indeed removed and placed into strategic locations across middle Europe. Hastings thought about his immediate surroundings being rural Scotland, and now the location had more of a significance now than ever before. Especially having visited the most important grave in Templar History and a simple marker stone in Switzerland, which had furnished him with some illicit and highly sensitive but more importantly accurate detail.

He now knew where a great amount of the Order's riches lay hidden. He knew that the public artefacts and riches were displayed in the many museums, churches and cathedrals globally and were accounted for, and the 'crème de la crème' the Scottish crown jewels and regalia, housed in the citadel, were marked.

But, it was not the public face of the Order that he was physically auditing, it was its inner framework of Christ's network, and an important inventory that was going to be giving him many restless and sleepless nights, and he also knew that soon the Vatican would become inquisitive and ask some rather serious searching questions.

Hastings was becoming progressively aware that he was touching the very fabric and tapestry of the Church. He knew he could be held accountable if he got things horribly wrong, and he also knew that past Knights from the Templar's Order had been put to the sword for greed and deceit.

He was certainly more than aware that many strange deaths occurred in the name of Christendom and he was convinced that he, Kemp Hastings of the Royal Lodge, was not going to become a biblical statistic, and was aware more than most mortals that the charitable Order we observe today is still as potent and volatile as it was back in its fledgling days.

And, any course of action for recourse would be deemed no different to having a 9mm bullet mounted in the back of the head or a sword thrust deep into one's gullet—an action executed by the Templars in order to dispense godly justice. Of course, that was if he or any other unscrupulous individual came too close for comfort in revealing to the outside world that the family silver was in fact 'war crime booty' or had been acquired under spurious circumstances, irrespective of which era it evolved from.

He took time and read the contents of the listed items on the secret inventory and the scroll that he had removed from its Swiss resting place, and of which, like most important things in the Order, lay under a mud pile under the watchful eye of the 'Suisse Grone Man'.

Hastings remained cognisant in his own mind where these many 'articles of faith' could be located. He then rolled out three scrolls on the table top and took a very deep breath indeed—that was before checking each item against its known recorded location.

Hastings pulled out an older map of Malta and quizzed the old Artillery ledger. He had lost count of the actual amount of cannon in the museum, or the coinage, but chose to make reference to the museum's holdings at the Grand Master's lodgings.

 Heilig-Holiest of Relics

Gold gilted roses—300
Ark Di Kovenant 2
Knocken—St Thomas—(Bones)—24
Knocken—St John—(Bones)—12
Kloth—(Burial Attire) 3 x lady saints—Magdalena, Magaretha & Bernadetti
Korpe—3 x Magdalena, Johann & Miriam
Kloth—Shroud Di Turin—1
Totenkopf—St Johann—1 (skull)
Totenkopf—St Magdalena—1 (skull)
Totenkopf—St Euphemia—Chalcedon—1 (skull)
Kistes—(caskets)—1,375 (mixed)
Konto—geld—128 billion
Krone—1 baum
Dokumenti Ekklesiastika—3,141,000
Kreuz—(true cross)—Acre (Bishop) 1 Acquired Hattin
Skrolls—Hammadi—222
Skrolls—Qumran—Essenes—852
Lancea Longini—1
Mahomet—statue—1
Calice Lapideum—stein Tasse—Dokumenti—Graal—1 (Troyes)
Schwert—9 (swords) Templeisen
Shields—9 Templeisen
Armour—6 Templeisen
116,500 Knights—interred globally—1128-2012

Hastings, poured himself a double sized brandy then closed the curtains to his modest accommodation and chilled out whilst deciding on what to do next—just as his HP laser scanner was busy flashing away.

CHAPTER TWENTY-THREE

'Double Entrende'

Erica Vine sat quietly in her red Volkswagen golf car reading some loose paperwork and was busy making notes about her meeting with the local journalist. Four hundred metres away, Kemp Hastings was making his way up the narrow street and walking briskly, having just crossed the stone bridge when he spied the red BMW exit from a side street. Then parked adjacent to Erica's vehicle.

Hastings grew instantly concerned and started walking more briskly, then found himself running towards the two parked cars. As he reached within two hundred metres, a single gunshot pierced his ears, and then the BMW sped off at an immense rate of knots up the narrow street.

Erica Vine was slumped over the car's steering wheel as he approached and having glanced into the car, he observed what he thought was a single bullet wound in her left temple that was already trickling blood down the Doctor's left side of her face.

Hastings began shouting at the top of his voice for help, and was confused, annoyed and scared. Why would anyone want to kill Erica? She was just an assistant. His emotions were all pulsing overtime and he was severely perplexed.

As he turned back towards Erica's car, he was confronted by what he thought was one of the BMW's German occupants, but only caught a glimpse of his face; the man who had suddenly appeared from nowhere, raised his hand up over his face.

The Colonel of the Teutonic order then raised his yellow pistol and shot a single round into the chest of Kemp Hastings. There was a moment of silence and nothingness, no sound, no feeling and no reality. The last thing Hastings remembered was his limp body being dragged into a nearby alley and left for the dogs.

The German Officer had dragged Hastings into the alleyway, and had flicked open his mobile phone just as the journalist appeared from the corner of the street. She had stopped dead in her tracks and was staring directly at the man's face. She then watched for a few seconds as the Volkswagen drove off at high speed up the street. The Officer then spun quickly on his heels and walked briskly away. Leaving the newspaper lady to make sense of what had just happened.

The journalist was momentarily awe struck. She watched as Hastings wriggled about on the floor in what appeared to her to be shear agony, thinking that he had suffered an attack of some kind.

She kneeled down and rolled him into the medical recovery position, stood up turned and fled to get assistance from somewhere, eventually stopping at a nearby shop doorway and grabbing the attention of the first person she came into contact with. She hastily explained what she thought she had just witnessed.

It was then that the pair returned to the scene and found Kemp Hastings leaning up against the alley wall. He was covered in dirt and had traces of blood trickling from his nose and his lower lip. He had obviously been assaulted or caught up in an entanglement with another aggressor—since the journalist had departed the scene to get help.

"Oh my goodness! It looks like he has been attacked even in the past few minutes!"

The journalist covered her mouth and almost wept in thinking as to what kind of person would take advantage of weakened person, let alone assault them enough to draw blood.

The cleric and the journalist began attempting to administer a certain level of first aid when the vicar spied the mobile phone. He picked up the Nokia, and hit the flashing keypad as he viewed the number.

Meanwhile, the journalist had dialled 999 to summon professional assistance. It was only after a few seconds and having closed the mobile phone that the cleric asked her to report a false alarm to the emergency services.

CHAPTER TWENTY-FOUR

Military Aid

T he Scottish army Colonel leaned over the body of Hastings and wiped his brow with a wet, cold cloth. The investigator flinched and drifted back and forth in and out of consciousness as the Officer dowsed him down with water and antiseptic ointment.

Every now and again the investigator would return back to reality for a short time, then fall off the planet in a fit of coughing and laughing. He had been severely drugged up and although he could hear many voices around him, he could not comprehend a single thing.

His assailant had shot him with a triple dose of hallucinogenic drugs, aiming straight at his vulnerable chest through his colourful waistcoat. Hastings was unsure whether or not the shot was a bullet or a dart; suffice to say it bloody hurt, and had sent him flying backwards and into a death curdling frenzy. He lay in an uncontrollable, intoxicated state, and lay in the alleyway for almost twelve minutes.

That was before being assisted by the local vicar and the news lady who was en route to the old Brechin Cathedral, and had stumbled across the journalist who had directed him towards Hastings as he bounced in and around the stone walled archway.

The priest had contacted the Order having found Hastings' mobile phone lying in the alley near to a few discarded buckets and boxes. The phone itself had been flicked open and the screen displayed speed dial two.

The Vicar had pressed the dial button and had found himself talking to a military Officer, who had instructed him to wait until help from another source appeared on the scene.

"Mr Hastings, can you hear me, old man? Can you try and grip my hand? Mr Hastings, it's me Colonel Marquis, we met a few days ago at the Grand Chaplain's funeral, try and squeeze my hand, Mr Hastings. Please no, no, Kemp, don't sleep, look at me buddy, you must not sleep my friend, and we need to find Miss Vine."

Hastings slowly but surely returned to a certain reality and his senses. The Colonel had been plying him with copious amounts of sweet coffee, black and laced with lots of honey and sugar. Within an hour so, Hastings eventually found himself sitting upright and almost fully engaged with the Colonel whilst eating a slice of heavily burnt toast.

"How the hell did I manage to get here?" He coughed and spluttered, although his head was buzzing and he felt very weak he still tried to stand up. The Colonel leaned over and gave him an encouraging hand of support, then sat him down.

"You are lucky to be alive, Mr Hastings. You had enough 'shit' in you to down an adult African elephant. Those Germans have just upped their game plan to stupidity level. I knew we should have taken the buggers out when we had the chance, but we also have orders to follow, sadly, it's a damn inconvenience. I am sure you understand, we can't go shooting all the enemy every second of the day."

Hastings rubbed his forehead then stretched his aching body upwards. He spied a few odd black and blue bruises and scuff marks on his arms; he had either been kicked around for a week or two by the All Nations rugby squad, and then dragged across some solid surface like the rocks of a volcano, or he had been involved in something far more sinister—he had no idea. He was hoping it was just the results from a confrontation with his not-so-nice German visitor. But, suffice to say, he felt sore and very sorry for himself, and vulnerable.

The Colonel brought him another cup of coffee, but more drinkable this time. He then fed him some more black toast and sweet shortcake, then tried to explain how he had been picked up by the Order.

"The quack says you're lucky to be alive my friend, if that churchy chap had not found you when he did, you could have pretty much ended—tits up in the gutter. The Doc injected you with some other shit into your veins to combat the settling effect; he says it should counteract your overdose. He also thinks it might have been a truth serum, a mixture of Temazepam and some other barbiturate type of drug."

Hastings looked up from his white, coffee mug, then spoke. "I saw Erica Vine, she had been shot in the head and was lying in her car as she waited for me. We were going to meet that journalist, then, I think I watched the BMW drive off, then, again I cannot be totally sure. I cannot remember much after that—it is all so damn ruddy hazy!" He stopped talking then shook his head slowly from side to side; his morale had been given a serious knock and he feared Madelyn could be next.

"The tall Krout, and so-called Colonel from the Wehrmacht or whatever Order he was from, he was the one who shot me."

The Colonel walked toward the doorway then stopped.

"I would not worry too much about Erica Vine, Mr Hastings, Our surveillance camera on the Lynx helicopter apparently caught Miss Vine's car being driven away from the scene of the so called incident, Your lovely Miss Vine was reported to have been driving.

We are not sure what is going on yet, but if you work to the fact that you have been hoodwinked for some reason, let alone drugged up to shit, then I think you should make this as advantageous as possible, and our visitors appear to have a new accomplice since arriving in our country—a female no less.

We thought she might be that journalist, Miss Crossgrave, but she appears to be less frumpy than Miss Vine according to the G2 Pilot that is. Oh! Incidentally, we have also found the BMW automobile in a car park in Edinburgh. It was vandalised, then torched, it was burnt out completely. We only recognised it because we had tagged it with a GPS chip. We have been following the German's activities since they arrived in the UK from Genoa last month."

The investigator stared on with hazy eyes and was suffering a headache from hell, and contemplated his next move. He now had the dilemma of determining whether or not Erica had been complicit in the charade of her own death; an action that had left him somewhat disturbed, let alone traumatised, confused and shot up on barbiturates, now only to find out that she was alive and kicking and part of some incomprehensible treasure plot.

The Colonel knew most of what was going on and had a far better spread of resources available to him, resources that Hastings was not accustomed to. He momentarily thought about his surroundings.

"Colonel Marquis can you do me a favour? Could you organise me a lift home please?" he asked, almost politely.

The reply was simple. "Indeed, Mr Hastings, we are here to serve the Order. Shall we say in an hour or so? I will get the pilot to warm up his chopper for you."

Hastings almost choked on his coffee and smirked at the Colonel's flippant statement, but his aching rib cage deterred him from any bouts of uncontrolled laughter. The Colonel clasped his hands, smiled back then left the room.

Hastings, meanwhile, called Madelyn at her home. It was now just after five in the afternoon and he was elated that she was waiting to hear from him. After a few minutes, he had explained his attack in the street and was trying to make sense of the attack.

Madelyn too, after a bit of time, had explained that she had received a cryptic text from Erica the previous morning, a text stating that she could not make the meeting with him because her car had been stolen and she was waiting for the police to visit and take a statement.

Erica also explained she had suffered a break in at her property, and that her mobile phone was still in the car and she did not have Hastings' number in her back up telephone. She was apparently more pissed off that her new iPod was also taken.

Hastings was looking a little confused, he thought they had already agreed to meet her at eleven o'clock anyway, perhaps he had been mistaken. And if that was the case then why was she there at the rendezvous thirty minutes too early, after all we are talking Erica, who was not exactly known as Miss Punctual.

He smelled a rat and it was reeking of jaeger schnitzel. He knew now that the meeting was a setup, but why? Maybe the intention was to drug him up then simply steal the inventory, but luckily for him the Colonel was on the ball and had acted swiftly, but that then meant that his home was empty. It was a plan to get him out of his home for a few hours.

"Shit! Bloody amateurs! You would think they would just kidnap me, and be done with it, but who was the new girl and why make Erica's death such a big charade, especially in the middle of the day. And, where was Erica now anyway?" That was the question he had to answer.

When Hastings arrived at the manse, he soon found his apartment had been totally trashed. The door had been simply smashed up and the door lock was in bits lying on the floor. There was not so much damage and vandalism to his property apart from the door lock, but the rest of the apartment showed signs of an orchestrated search.

All the drawers to the various cabinets had been emptied onto the sofa; his book shelf was literally cleared and all his favourite reads were splattered across the living space. What made things worse was that his fridge had also been cleared out and the open cartons of cream, orange and milk lay tipped across the black, granite kitchen tops.

He was annoyed and pissed off at the same time. He could not call the police because there was no way he wanted to have them snooping around as he was in the middle of a sensitive audit. But instead called Madelyn's mobile; well, he would have spoken to Madelyn if he had hit the correct dialling buttons, but instead in is anger and confusion he had hit Erica's number instead.

"Hello," answered the voice of a woman at the other end, but it was not Erica. He just listened as he tried to interpret any noises that would identify where the voice was located. He checked the number then realised he had cocked up.

"Ah, hello Erica, it's me, how are you? Can we meet?" he offered, then waited and listened intently concentrating on what he could pick up from the background noises. He heard a distant feint voice and it was definitely not Scottish.

He knew the language was German, he recognised the taller Officer's deeper tones. He knew there and then that the trio were responsible for the break in at Erica's flat and they had managed to get into Erica's phone, and that meant they most likely had access to her iPad and emails.

His gut started to churn as he thought about two men terrorising Erica in her flat and he wiped a single tear from his eye. Hastings flicked the mobile phone closed.

Grabbing his keys, he left his flat and headed for Erica's apartment.

Twenty minutes later and Hastings was knocking on Erica's front door and was in a clear panic.

"Erica, it's me, Kemp, let me in," he shouted, whilst knocking on the door and trying the door handle. He swore he saw the door curtain move at one of the lower corners, then he heard the safety lock being unhinged.

The door opened slowly and Erica stood staring at him. Hastings saw fear in her eyes and she had obviously been crying, her hair was a mess and she was still shaking as she stood in her jogging suit.

"Hey, girl, are you alright? Madelyn told me you had a break in, are you really okay? I mean you are not hurt are you. Do you need a doctor or nurse?"

Erica closed the door and led him into the kitchen where she handed him a newspaper cutting, then folded her arms across her body.

"You and your damned coins and gold bullion, I told you they would bring shit . . . those bastards tied me up and they stole my bloody car. And, the ruddy police, waste of time, a complete set of insensitive morons. Do you know, they have absolutely no idea about how to deal with people? Especially when dealing with the victims who are upset. Bloody ignoramuses the lot of them, that's what they are—fkin . . . useless. Do you know what one officer actually said to me, he intimated that I had instigated the whole thing, accusing me of bringing those idiots back to my flat after a night at the pub, cheeky bast . . ."

She momentarily controlled her anger and was pointing to the newspaper cutting. It was an article regarding the lost Templar Treasure. "Look, last year when we discovered those swords and those little gold fish trinkets, well, those fish were part of another consignment of riches that had been stolen from the museum in Koln two years ago. There was also a bunch of German wartime Reichsbank gold coins, but I do not recall seeing any coins do you, Kemp?"

Hastings rubbed his chin, then spoke. "No, I didn't but Magnus Carter from the Fisher Kings office, he says that some coins were found, don't think he mentioned our batch of 1,500 though."

"So what now?" she asked, as Hastings gave her a quick hug to calm her down.

"Well, Erica, there is something you should know: when I went to meet you and Jennifer yesterday . . ." Hastings stopped talking and held his chest. He stopped and leaned slightly forward as a shooting pain began running up through his rib cage. Erica also leaned forward and placed a hand at the back of his shoulder.

"It's you I think I should be asking if you are okay, not you asking me, you big ape. What have you been up to anyway?"

Hastings stood upright as the pain eased off and explained his recent encounter with his visitors.

"Those Krouts had done an elaborate head job on me. When I was walking up Bridge Street to meet you yesterday, I saw you, or who I thought was you sitting in your car. Then I saw a sight that scared the living shit out of me—you had been shot in the head by the driver of the BMW, and incidentally, they have a new, silver Mercedes now apparently. Anyway you were slumped over the steering wheel of your VW when I looked into it, and then, when I turned around to see what was behind me, that cheeky, tall bastard German shot me right in the middle of the chest with enough drugs to drop a rhino."

Erica leaned over the counter and located a tall glass, then filled it with fresh orange juice, and offered it to him. "Here, take this, I have some pain killers somewhere."

Hastings carried on. "Well, Erica, that's not it all, the vicar from the chapel says he was told by a girl that I had been bouncing around in the alley, it was your journalist friend, and for some reason I cannot get it out of my head that she may have something to do with this. Maybe I am paranoid, but . . ."

Erica walked through to the adjacent room and returned with a yellow Taser gun.

"I think this is what might have been one of the weapons that was used on you. Found it this morning when I was clearing up the mess from yesterday."

Hastings held the weapon in his hands and found it quite heavy to hold. He gave it the cursory once over and observed that the all the identity markings had been removed. Apart from the charging socket which had clearly been marked with a red sticker stating: 'Warning—harmful to children', the Taser was clean. He placed the pistol on the table and turned toward Erica.

"You will need to get out of here for a while. Those morons have trashed my flat. They were looking for documents that will lead them to their treasure of World War II, bloody idiots, they have no idea that this gold was melted down in 1976 with a shed of other items. They might return and see what they can recover. I would say stay at mine bit they will be watching. There is a safe house at this address."

He then passed Erica a piece of paper with the address of the reservoir and a contact number written upon it.

"Erica, we the Order, control most of what these guys do. You will be in safe hands. Find Colonel Marquis and tell him I sent you, he will know what to do."

CHAPTER TWENTY-FIVE

'Academic Encounter'

Kemp Hastings sat and watched out the small arched window that overlooked the modest garden area of the manse. He huffed a little then rubbed his chin. His mobile had begun vibrating as it sat on the table top and startled him. He was momentarily reminded of reality as he gazed into the countryside. Just as he drifted off into a moment of deep thought, he stared at the mobile and let it ring a further two rings before picking it up then listened to the voice at the other end.

The voice was soft and smooth. "Mr Hastings, good morning, I am the chief archivist of the Scottish historical records office, in Edinburgh, and I have been asked to contact you by one of our mutual friends. Our mutual colleague says that you are searching for some internal detail on our Order—information regarding some old dusty boxes—is this correct?"

Hastings waited and took note of the telephone number. He did not recognise it but the voice seemed genuine enough, no indicators of anxiety or haste in the tone and spot on regarding the subject matter.

"Sorry, I missed your name. Can you tell me what is it again?" asked Hastings. The voice at the other end answered with an academic and clinical response as any normal archivist would, and also with an air of command and authority. Then, there was an air of expectancy from the caller, a pause in their conversation; it was as if the recipient was waiting to hear a further barrage of about three million questions.

Requests for information and answers that would be asked, and of which would normally lead to a further million information snippets alluding to more conversations that somehow were inextricably threaded to the original request or question.

"Oh, pardon me, Mr Hastings, it's Brodie, James Brodie, Ex Deacon of the St Thomas's foundational church. I have been working with the late archivist of the Angus archives Dr Toadie, he had mentioned your name several times in our many conversations, it was from him I got your telephone number from. Hope you don't mind?"

Hastings paused for a few seconds and listened, he then walked through his modest apartment and found Freddy's letter; the communication was still sitting on the side cabinet near to his piano.

He listened intently to the archivist as he explained that since the incident at the priory there had been an acute amount of interest in the archives relating to local church records and testimonials left by visiting church members, but he was very concerned that a very unhealthy interest was being driven toward the priory itself.

Brodie explained that the Ministry of Education's, Chief Records Officer had also been killed in a bizarre car accident just a few weeks prior. Ironically, it was after he announced that his new novel contained details of a World War II treasure trail cover up, and it was going to disclose the whereabouts of Hitler's so called hidden or secret bank records and diary extracts, and had intimated that enclosed within the ledgers he had found more modern accounts and reports that pin pointed actual members of the government cabinet and influential, international figures who had been systematically involved in moving great wealth around the planet between 1945 and 1986.

Suffice to say that Dr Toadie's demise was considered part of an orchestrated cover plan to remove any leads that stemmed back to a particular German or British foundation. Hastings listened and absorbed what Brodie was telling him before speaking.

"So, tell me what do you want from me, Mr Brodie?" he asked, then waited for an answer.

"Well, I have discovered some rather interesting photographs that were taken about 1946 and again in the year 1977, at a placed called Toplitz, Bavaria. Have you ever heard of a place called Berchesgaden, Mr Hastings?" Brodie continued without leaving a pause for Hastings to answer. "Well, there are seven photographs in total. There is also a note written on one picture from some army Colonel who states that the pictures were taken by an army contingent that intercepted a so called convoy that was being prepared for despatch.

There are some banquet photographs also with various members posing for a photograph which included British and American soldiers. But interestingly enough there are also receipts and copies of Swiss banking details signed by what appears to be a British consulate representative, dated 1944."

The phone then went very quiet as Hastings fumbled about in his satchel for a beige coloured envelope. He knew he had seen a letter in the bag, a brief from Bern with the Swiss post mark that resembled a consulate insignia, and one that depicted a double headed eagle, clearly embossed with a Wehrmacht logo, which he thought contained just a seating plan for a function. Maybe this was the reason for the meeting.

In his immediate assumptions, he had been correct. The letter was indeed a planned seating plan, but this seating plan was a primary sit down get together with the very Officers and gentlemen who had engineered the movement of some heavy duty bullion across middle Europe. Not only in 1945, but up until the late 80's.

"Can we meet, Mr Brodie? I have a letter that you may be interested in, and, I would also like to view those pictures you have."

After an agreement was reached, the two men had arranged to meet somewhere neutral and out of sight of the Teutonic order and definitely far away from any mainstream city.

Brodie had requested a meeting at a rural village of Glen Finnan, a small country hamlet that sits in the highlands of Scotland. Hastings knew the towered monument at the head of Loch Shiel would have several visitors and they would blend in quite nicely. Then he thought about the weather. He looked up.

"Shitty rain, best bring a brolly my friend, you are going to need one."

Chase

Hastings stepped on to the train and found a seat facing the direction of travel. He preferred to see what was coming toward him as opposed to what scenery was whizzing by his eye line. He opened his magazine and absorbed an article that explained a new discovery about some relics and bones that had been discovered in what is modern day Jordan, and could have belonged to the very late John the Baptist.

"Well, that will keep the conspiracy theorists at work for a while, the crusades are littered with so called authenticate relics," he muttered, then read the complete article before, playing with his mobile phone.

After about an hour into the journey, Hastings was disturbed as a man sat opposite him placed a single gold coin on the table top. Hastings glanced at the coin and then looked at its owner.

"Mr Hastings, you are a difficult man to pin down. My name is Brodie. How are you?"

The man offered a hand for shaking.

"I thought you might have got on this train, I mean, Glen Finnan, it's quite a bit away!"

The Deacon did not smile but was staring beyond the interconnecting door to the adjoining rail carriage.

"I will be hopping off at next station, keep getting this feeling that I am being stalked, and recently I have been receiving the oddest set of texts and emails, from God knows where, anyway here you go, did you bring the photos?"

Just as the Deacon passed a beige coloured envelope across the table the train took a sudden jolt and the lights flickered as the train began slowing down.

"Shit!" remarked the Deacon, as the train shuddered to an almost squealing stop. "We need to flee my friend, this just might be our first and last meeting, I fear," he said, then passed another small package to Hastings. "Get this to the Order, and get off this bloody train quickly. If you don't hear from me in 24 hours then I . . ." Brodie cut off and hit the electronic 'door open' button, then waited impatiently as nothing happened. He turned and watched on, just as two figures appeared in the distant carriage and had started walking toward them from the far end of the long passenger train. He extracted a tool from his pocket and twisted the key in the hydraulic lock, the door eased open with a low hiss, and, he jumped instantly into the darkness of the night.

Hastings wasted no time and followed in his footsteps. He was unsure if they had been seen talking together or not by the two uninvited guests. But he scrambled his way out of the small station and headed in to the adjacent forest for cover.

After several minutes of country landscape negotiation, Hastings was lost. He found himself in a forest clearing and was searching desperately for the Deacon who had momentarily vanished into the hinterland.

"Bastard, what was Brodie thinking about, setting me up like that, no, no, no, this is not good, what a pain in the arse," he said out loud, just as the gun shots whizzed overhead. Hastings automatically ducked down and scrambled through the undergrowth; his mind had toggled straight back into squaddie and survival mode. He took little time and found a gulley that ran southwards. He rolled into to the recess, then lay flat and started easing himself along the leafy assault course. After a few minutes, he had crawled its full length, then he stopped and observed ahead.

About one hundred metres away, he thought he saw a lone figure lurking in the shadows of the trees, he was correct, the gunman was slowly jostling from one strategic firing point to the next. He was searching for his new found quarry!

As Hastings squinted his gaze, he could see the silhouette of the shooter in the veiled light of the moon. He spied the steam slowly bellowing up from the smoking barrel of the gun as the hot air mixed with the cold damp atmosphere.

Hastings froze in his fox hole, and watched on as he wrestled with the confused mix of undergrowth, weeds, brambles and tree branches, and waited patiently whilst anticipating running for deeper cover and had weighed up where the next bullet was going to end up.

The rifleman then shot a few sporadic shots somewhere deep into the forest. Hastings knew he was relatively still safe as long as he lay very low and quiet. The rifleman shot off a few other rounds in the wrong direction, then paused to re-load.

Hastings was breathing erratically, his brow was dripping tiny droplets of sweat enriched with his acidic body fluid that ran into his eyes causing a stinging sensation to distract and annoy him; he fought back the urge to wipe his brow until it was absolutely safe to do so.

As he waited very patiently, he could smell his own body odour creeping up through his clothing and he slowly wiped under his arms with his hand—any erratic movement now would be suicidal. It was now almost two o'clock in the morning and he was saturated in his own body fluid, mainly from his running activities and now by his sweat driven fear.

His hair had become sticky and matted and he knew he had at least two days growth of beard on his chiselled jaw. Being on the run was not a predicament or a position that he was accustomed to being in, but everything had suddenly became so bloody awkward and he was annoyed to say the least.

He muttered a hail of disappointment to himself, having lost his mobile telephone either dropping it somewhere between jumping from the train or tramping through the thick undergrowth in the dense forest.

"And where the hell was here anyway?" he asked himself.

He knew he was somewhere in the Scottish wilderness, lost between Glencoe or the Great Glen and normal civilisation. The train had been travelling for at least one and a half hours before the deranged treasure seekers had materialised. Either way, he was now on foot and was marching headlong into the dark wet undergrowth of the conifers.

Having found his safe haven and another hiding hole, he had sat down and was watching on with the intent of not doing very much. The gun shots had ceased, the world around him had fallen into an eerie kind of silence apart from the nocturnal activities of the local wildlife.

An owl hooted from somewhere deep inside the trees alerting him not to sleep, he tried standing up, his legs ached his back was giving him discomfort and the rain had started to cast another unwelcomed wet blanket over the canopy above him.

He gently reached over a heavy branch, grasped a strong limb of a tree and pulled himself to his feet, then started looking for any signs of a track or pathway or clearing. Eventually, he spied a small trail of flattened bracken bushes and moved stealthily towards what he thought was a light at the far end of the copse.

Overhead, he swore he heard the hum of the gems two twin turbines of the Lynx helicopter in the far distance. He knew that noise travels farther at night, maybe not so far especially in these mountainous regions of the highlands, let alone being suppressed by the thick trees.

The high pitched tone was indeed the chopper but it was flying away from his immediate location, the aircraft was being flown by the army Colonel Graham Marquis at the controls, and his passenger a dignitary of some significant standing. And not just any VIP either, this was Britain's number three politician, the Secretary of State for Defence. A planned encounter with the Temple and who had been entertaining himself and his friends amongst the Highland clan chiefs in the company and guest of the Earl of Mar.

Hastings wiped his brow, then swept back his hair and started ghost walking through the trees again, when after a few seconds a higher pitched tone rattled his earshot and he instantly fell to his knees knowing full well that the high pitch tone belonged to a specific piece of military sniper hardware.

And scarily enough it was being energised for use, the signature tone of an optical night device he knew only too well, having had a close relationship with his own dedicated laser intensified suet sight a few years prior.

A must have technical tool for would be killers and for any respectable squaddie yomping the streets of Ireland, searching for mortar base plates or IEDs at night, searching for weapons that were going to kill or maim innocent people. The night sight was now his worst enemy.

'Oh, what joys,' he thought to himself. His army days in the province suddenly came back to haunt him, and it had just reminded him of his last encounter with one.

Too many years ago, now, he had to think carefully, and calmly, then he quietly sat down on the ground and hugged a few branches nearby, hoping that the foliage would provide some camouflage or adequate protection.

An eternity of time had lapsed, it was easily ten minutes and he was still trying to hold his breath, struggling in pain whilst remaining calm, trying not to budge a single inch that could alert any potential assassins in the vicinity.

His tactics had obviously worked so far, but that was until he then caught the sound of more footsteps stomping across the brittle bracken and fern undergrowth nearby, the twigs and branches cracking underfoot sending clear signals that the visitor was now moving away from him. He breathed out very deeply.

Somehow he had evaded the infra-red sighting system and knew full well it would be attached to its dedicated deadly assault rifle, a magazine installed with a few bullets which could have had his name etched across their brass 7.62 full metal jackets.

Seven point six two self-loading rifle, or SLR, the backbone weapon of the pre-nineties British army soldier. If you were lucky enough, and strongly built, you got furnished with the LMG, the light machine gun. 'Light!' thought Hastings, 'It weighed a bloody ton . . .'

A powerful weapon, the SLR, and perhaps the British Army's best assault rifle. Weighing in at nine point nine pounds, the weapon was a considerable tool to have in one's arsenal, a certifiable technical killer. Hastings took another very deep breath as the shadow disappeared from his view.

After a few more minutes, he started walking in the opposite direction to his contemporary foe. He walked on, remaining consistent in his stride and eventually met a track that led to the black top roadway a few hundred metres away.

As he broke the forest's southern tree line, he spied the big, old moon sitting high in the sky and doing pretty much nothing apart from casting a nocturnal array of light upon the landscape. He walked towards the roadway, and headed north.

Seven hours later and having hitched a ride more than twenty miles, Hastings found himself sitting in the foyer of the local pub waiting for his trusty assistant to join him. He had spent a good part of the morning evading most people and cars that came into the small village, but none of them belonged to Deacon Brodie.

Madelyn had driven to the small village having followed Hastings' explicit instructions to the letter. He had entrusted her with a fistful of ecclesiastical documents and had made himself a deliberate decoy. They had met at the designated rendezvous point near the old derelict church building, then he swapped his green, army back pack for a red leather satchel.

As Madelyn and Hastings waited for Erica to arrive at the lodge, they had learned from the radio that a body had just been discovered in the nearby forest and that police were treating the incident as very suspicious although the news reader stated that it could have been a hunting incident. Hastings shuffled uneasily in his chair on hearing the news.

"These damn idiots have gone way beyond their call of duty. They have killed, I think, three people so far, and I think we had all better split up again. You had better not contact me for the next couple of days. When you get back to Dundee, lie low. I will contact you. Take care and I will see you both very soon. I have to call in a few favours, this audit may have to include a trail of dead bodies and they will not be ours, that much I will guarantee you. Tell Erica, she was right."

After an hour or so both girls had a quick lunch and had departed the sleepy village.

Hastings had jumped the train and was sitting eighty miles away with a pint of lager and his thoughts. That was when the Grand Prior sat next to him and ordered a cup of lemon tea.

"Kemp, how are you? You look a bit tired. I hear you have had some interesting cross country excursions."

Hastings wiped his brow and huffed. "You could say that, nearly never made it this far, they shot the other archivist Deacon Brodie last night. This cannot go on. These people are just murdering thugs."

The Grand Prior was nodding in agreement and thanked the waitress for his cup of lemon tea. "Well, we will just have to bring things to an end rather abruptly then, shan't we? Oh, by the way, I would like you to accompany me to the Kirk next door.

I suppose I should show you, now, what all this excitement is about, it's not just that fistful of coins and bullion I showed you, we have something a wee bit more interesting than that. c'mon walk with me brother"

Having consumed their coffee and tea, Kemp Hastings stood side by side with the Grand Prior in the second vault of the Church of Mary Magdalene.

Hasting's gaze was resting upon one hundred, gold-clad boxes. Each box was encrusted with jewels beyond his wild imagination and stacked three deep. Sitting off to one corner sat thirty-six Wehrmacht crates of what appeared to be old world war II ammunition boxes. Hastings recognised them straight away: this was part of the Toplitz treasure heist no doubt about it.

The Grand Prior handed Kemp Hastings, of the Royal Lodge, a single heavy iron door key.

"It's all yours now, I am afraid, I have other churches and coffers to hand over. I am to move abroad with our Order; they need a liaison Officer for the Vatican."

Hastings stared at the key, then stared at the Grand Prior in bewilderment. "What am I supposed to do with this lot?" he asked, expecting the Grand Prior to hand him a ledger or at least sign some sort of handover certificate.

"Two things Brother Hastings. Firstly, add this lot to your audit list, add say £1.2 billion in physical assets to the physical inventory. Secondly, spend what you need to, and if you want a new house buy one, but just add the deeds to that pile over there in the corner, otherwise, life is good from here on in. But we still have to deal with the unwanted attention."

An hour or so later, Hastings had called the visiting pseudo Teutonic Monks and arranged to with meet them in order to bring this murderous charade to a final conclusion.

The next morning as Kemp Hastings sat behind the wheel of the Jaguar car in the local car park, and was contemplating his next course of action, when the first bullet struck the top of the windscreen of his prized crimson possession.

The bullet had hit the framework in a splurt of muffled splatter; there was the initial thump followed by a series of cracking and rippling noises as the plate of laminated glass in front of him disintegrated into a raft of a million tiny crystal sharp cubes.

He instantly ducked down to the left side of the steering wheel and shielded his eyes just as the second shot echoed in a muffled dolt a few inches above his head as it struck the door post, momentarily aiding what was left of the wind shield to fall inwards, showering him in yet another zillion more fragments of razor sharp shards.

A sudden, cold fear caught the moment as Hastings battled with the passenger door's locking mechanism. Then after two desperate attempts to open the door, the spring loaded release latch activated. He then slid out of the car on his belly and escaped from the confines of the Jaguar, soon finding himself scurrying into a nearby doorway, slouching down and keeping very low.

He heard the distinct report of a larger weapon coming from very nearby. It was definitely coming from behind him. 'Shit,' he thought. He had been surrounded, the sound almost resembling what he would describe as a high velocity rifle shot.

He feared his worst and made ready to do or die. Then he heard another shot ring out, then another clearly, again from a more solid weapon more of a heavy rifle report than that of a hand pistol. As he glanced up the alleyway, he spied the Mar Atholl's army, one-man killing machine marching heading towards him.

As the Colonel raised his rifle for the third time into a sniper's shoulder position in order to take another shot, which was complimented incidentally with a fly-by as the Lynx battle-configured, attack helicopter flew overhead. It was just then that the officer began waving his arms directly at Hastings, intimating for him to 'get down on the ground and stay there'.

Hastings got to his knees as another volley of four shots whizzed by his left ear, then echoed as a series of soft thuds a hundred feet or so away; followed by a muffled dolt as each of the bullets found their destined targets.

Colonel Marquis took several more steps forward with his rifle clearly trained on the two bodies that now lay in two limp masses of flesh and bone on the roadway, each lifeless and very dead, approximately seventy metres or so away. He then stopped in his tracks and waited.

Hastings watched on in total bewilderment, and almost felt himself smile in sheer delight to see the face of the 'pompous ass' Officer staring back at him, as he lowered his rifle.

"You see, Mr Hastings, that's what happens when you let people know what hell is going on around you, or at least tell them where you are located, you see, if we know what you are up to! we can simply send in the Cavalry—just when you need us most. Miss Linn obviously does not want to lose you just yet either, you lucky sod"

The Colonel offered him a helping hand up, then they both walked towards the parked silver Mercedes. The Colonel took out a handkerchief from his inside jacket pocket and wiped the sweat from his brow then spoke.

"Fanatics, these bloody people, thinking they could just inflict terror or mayhem across Scottish soil, but today and sadly for them, just is not happening, I am afraid. Did you know these two activists are part of an underworld construct, an element of anarchists that has sworn to strike fear amongst normal, decent people, like you and I? Bloody far left wingers, almost verging on Neo-Nazism ideals, and a very sad sign of the times.

Hastings pondered on the Colonel's comments, 'Mmmh', normal, decent people and he, the Colonel, had just shot two men in cold blood in a horrific gun fight.

"God," he muttered, and nodded as he agreed with the Colonel's comments.

The Colonel then rubbed the gun sight of his trusted rifle.

"Goodness, Mr Hastings, the good Lord above won't let these idiots repeat their warring ways. We can't have mayhem running riot without permission from the establishment. Anyway that is all our worries over for today, done and dusted—as they say, well, at least, for now."

Hastings stopped and gazed back at the Jaguar car that was literally peppered with a few large bullet holes and supported no windscreen. His prize possession; a car that almost became his unplanned shrine. He wiped his own brow of sweat, then spoke.

"So, tell me, Colonel, how did you know where I was? You said Miss Linn?"

The Officer clicked the safety mechanism on his assault rifle and placed it by his side.

"Three things, Mr Kemp Hastings, firstly, we tagged your little, red Noddy car over there with a locator beacon, a magnetic newer version of GPS unit; and secondly, you have some very caring, remarkable and very good friends, namely Miss Madelyn Linn; and thirdly, and perhaps more importantly, the 'Grand Master', he said that he wanted you kept alive and protected until you have completed your inventory check and conducted your important audit.

The Grand Master also said something that I am not quite too sure what it actually means. But he said 'quote' to be sure to remind you to return 'your book' on medieval armour back to the library!"

Giving out an involuntary cough and splutter of laughter, Hastings placed a hand in his jacket pocket and re-assured himself that the 'Templari Thesaurus' was still in his possession. He then placed a hand on the shoulder of the Officer and said politely.

"Well, Colonel, what can I say, thank you seems to be so insignificant. I mean you have saved my sorry ass twice now, and I still have no idea who is really pulling all the strings."

The colonel smiled back at him, 'Agnus Dei Mister Hastings Agnus Dei, your time will come. It's not just yet!'

The Colonel then removed his mobile telephone from his pocket and answered the incoming call. He paused for a few moments longer, and smiled again then suddenly passed the mobile telephone to Hastings and walked away.

The voice at the other end was not a voice he recognised, it was a clearly an aristocratic, upper crust tone. He thought for a split second of an Etonian or an English Oxford education; Scottish overtones and the vocabulary was concise, clean and very direct.

Hastings listened for a few moments longer, then answered. "Yes, your highness, I am sure I can look into that particular subject over the next couple of days, for you, and thank you."

Hastings closed the mobile phone and stared back at the Colonel, who then spoke. with an air of authority. "People and friends in high places, eh!"

A moment's pause for further reflection, as the Colonel spoke again. "Oh, and by the way, old chap, you perhaps need to get an Aston Martin, Mr Hastings—that air conditioning on your Jaguar just simply won't do."

Both men shared a rare moment of laughter as they watched Erica Vine and Madelyn Linn walk slowly towards them both.

End

Afterword

All items termed as 'the Orders inventory' are maintained under the rightful ownership of the establishment as—'Knights Templar signature pieces' and therefore, must be remain secure and safe at all times.

The reader should fully acknowledge that such objects must be secreted away from both prying eyes and potential unscrupulous thieves whilst being managed under a control process that the Order has religiously conducted chronologically for the past seven centuries or more, and again of which, the process has proven to be a very effective method of inventory control to date.

The author acknowledges at this juncture that being the custodian of any such holy or important artefact is not a task of custody that is taken lightly by any of the members of the internal Order, and, of which, their duties are executed with clear and concise understanding of both routines and stewardship, and often under a blanket of scrutiny overseen by the keepers. There is a great deal of personal self sacrifice as custodians of such wonderful objects and it is appreciated by those who manage business.

The custody processes and actions which have been set appropriately in place are to ensure that custody of such items assigned to individuals by the holy order 'are never' exposed to unscrupulous entities and that, the security measures applied to their protection are adequately robust enough to be manipulated by the inner conclave of the Knights Templar Order where practical

Therefore, in an attempt to maintain an appropriate level of context for this work of 'fiction' the author has limited his attentions to a mere 200 years time frame and has taken a literal 'snapshot' from the year 1812 to modern day 2012, stemming back only two centuries.

And, as a pre cursor to publishing this work, the author had been granted a limited amount of access to internal libraries or archives which hold documents and records—not normally afforded to impromptu storytellers or reporters in general, again, the author respectfully thanks individuals who have 'opened the doors to the dusty boxes whilst lifting the various lids to 14th century coffers' and thus, contributed to this important notional account of modern day Templar activity.

Historical 'ethos'

The ancient Knights Templar Order of the 12th century era has indeed been steeped in myths, legends, folklore and many mysterious stories have added a tremendous amount of analytical fuel for modern media and scholars to shape their many fantasy books, films and documentaries upon. Therefore, solidifying the existence of this revered religious order since the year 1119 and onwards into the present day where the Order has not gone un-noticed.

Why The Knights' Templar as an institution has such a fundamental standing on the global stage is very much open to debate. But it is very clear from the many archival records that 'The Knights Templar' were involved in preserving something which cannot simply be purchased, traded or even bantered for in the common marketplace—and is perhaps something that is far greater than mere gold and shiny trinkets.

This inexplicable link to many myths, fantasies and legends have bonded the Knights' Templar ethos and fabric solidly together as it rippled through time and history, penetrating deep into the very social framework of our modern day 21st century faith itself.

This belief has permeated through modern society with such potency that it has been firmly embedded by it's shear popularity alone; albeit supported by a fistful of clandestine esoterical meanings and symbology carefully laid within its complex interwoven tapestry.

The Knights' Templar Order we observe today in the 21st century are indeed alive and kicking globally and unlikely to change the way they hav

fundamentally functioned for the past 723 years, and of which, can be easily located by a simple web search as previously stated.

As a collective 'Brotherhood in arms', the poor knights had never actually left the structure of society, but ran more 'silently' in the ever changing background, and of course still do, the Order controlling or advising the modern commercial world we observe today—depending on one's personal outlook. preserving the memory of the bravest eight Knights who shed their blood across the many battlefields of Christendom.